'Brillia[...]
and ge[...]ing'
M.G. Leon[...], author of *Beetle Boy*

'Full of heart and humour,
wit and wisdom'
Sophie Anderson, author of
The House With Chicken Legs

'So good
you'll CLUCK with laughter!'
Pamela Butchart, author of
Baby Aliens Got My Teacher!

'Wonderfully heart-warming
and absolutely hilarious'
Catherine Doyle, author of
The Storm Keeper's Island

'Will have readers
snorting with giggles'
Northern Echo

'A gloriously fun, madcap
adventure with a celebration
of friendship at its heart.'
Anna James, author of *Pages & Co:
Tilly and the Bookwanderers*

'Hysterically funny!'
Jeremy Strong

Books by Sam Copeland

CHARLIE CHANGES INTO A CHICKEN

CHARLIE TURNS INTO A T-REX

PUFFIN BOOKS

Sam Copeland is an author, which is an enormous shock to him. He is from Manchester and now lives in London with two smelly cats, three smelly children and one relatively clean-smelling wife. Sam also work as a mammoth shaver, shaving mammoths so they can hide peacefully among elephants without being bothered by nosy scientists. *Charlie Morphs Into a Mammoth* is his third book, following *Charlie Changes Into a Chicken* and *Charlie Turns Into a T-Rex*. Despite legal threats, he refuses to stop writing.

SAM COPELAND

CHARLIE

MORPHS
INTO A

MAMMOTH

ILLUSTRATED BY
SARAH HORNE.

PUFFIN

PENGUIN BOOKS

UK | USA | Canada | Ireland | Australia
India | New Zealand | South Africa

Penguin Books is part of the Penguin Random House group of companies
whose addresses can be found at global.penguinrandomhouse.com.

www.penguin.co.uk
www.puffin.co.uk
www.ladybird.co.uk

Penguin
Random House
UK

First published 2020

001

Text copyright © Sam Copeland, 2020
Illustrations copyright © Sarah Horne, 2020

The moral rights of the author and illustrator have been asserted

Text design by Janene Spencer
Printed in Great Britain by Clays Ltd, Elcograf S.p.A.

A CIP catalogue record for this book is available from the British Library

ISBN: 978–0–241–34623–5

All correspondence to
Penguin Books
Penguin Random House Children's
80 Strand, London WC2R 0RL

MIX
Paper from
responsible sources
FSC® C018179

Penguin Random House is committed to a
sustainable future for our business, our readers
and our planet. This book is made from Forest
Stewardship Council® certified paper.

To Mum –
thanks for always making sure
I had a book in my hand.

DO NOT TOUCH!

THIS BOOK IS THE PROPERTY OF ....

MY AGE IS ....

I LIVE IN ....

MY FAVOURITE AUTHOR IS ...Sam Copeland............................

WHEN YOU PICK BOGEYS, DO YOU
A) EAT THEM *OR*
B) WIPE THEM UNDER TABLES AND BEHIND SOFAS?

....

WHICH OF YOUR PARENTS FARTS THE MOST? ....

AT WHAT AGE DO YOU BECOME AN OLD PERSON? ....

WHAT IS THE MEANING OF LIFE? ....

WOULD YOU RATHER HAVE TWO NOSES OR THREE BUMS?

....

IF YOU WERE WITH YOUR FAMILY AT BUCKINGHAM PALACE AND
YOU FARTED NEAR THE QUEEN, WHICH FAMILY MEMBER WOULD
YOU TRY AND BLAME IT ON?

....

AND IF YOU WERE WITH YOUR FAMILY AT BUCKINGHAM PALACE
AND THE QUEEN FARTED NEAR YOU AND SHE TRED BLAMING IT
ON YOU, WOULD YOU TAKE THE BLAME?

....

A FEW LETTERS FROM OUR
VALUED READERS CONCERNING
THE LAST BOOK

Dear Puffin Books,

WHAT?? Where were the T-Rexes?!
I spent the last of my pocket money
on *Charlie Turns Into a T-Rex* and
I feel completely cheated.

Worst wishes,
Josh, nine, Whitstable

Dear Puffin Books,

I should have learned my lesson after the first book, when Charlie didn't change into a chicken. But I didn't. Instead, I bought *Charlie Turns Into a T-Rex* fully expecting him to turn into a Tyrannosaurus. Once again, I was lied to. I shall never trust Sam Copeland, Puffin Books or, in fact, anybody ever again.

Yours devastatedly,
Mae Dupname, ten,
Banjax-on-Thames

Dear Puffin Books,

No T-Rex?! That's the worst news. The worst. Sneaky Sam Copeland is a stone-cold loser! I could write a children's book better than him. Easy!
Yours,
D. Trump, 73 and ¾, USA

Puffin Books
80 Strand
London

Dear Reader,

Well, here we are again.

After a string of letters from angry children from around the world complaining about the non-appearance of T-Rexes in *Charlie Turns Into a T-Rex*, we have put in place measures to ensure that the author inserts WITHOUT FAIL at least one mammoth into this book.

Please find below a written-down, 100% guaranteed, cross-your-heart-and-hope-to-die, unbreakable promise from the author.

Yours faithfully,
The Publisher

Dear Puffin Books and Angry Children Around the World,

I TOTALLY, 100% promise that Charlie will turn into a mammoth in this book.

Your truthful author,
Sam Copeland

CHAPTER 1

Charlie McGuffin was late again.

And he really couldn't be late this time or he was a dead man.

And what was Charlie McGuffin late for?

That's an *excellent* question, dear reader. You all seem like a clever bunch, not like that dreadful crowd who read the last two books. They were *awful*. I think you guys are going to be my favourite readers so far – I can feel it in my bones.

So, in answer to your question:

Charlie McGuffin couldn't be late for his school trip or he was a dead man.

And where was the school trip to?

1

Another great question, you clever reader! Well done! The school trip was to the local zoo.

And was he actually going to be *dead* if he was late?

No! Of course he wasn't! Now that was a silly question. I meant he'd just be in quite a lot of trouble.

You know, we got off to a good start, reader, but I'm beginning to have my doubts.

So, to be clear – Charlie McGuffin couldn't be late for his school trip or he was a dead (not *actually* dead) man.

Oh, *come* ON. What is wrong with you? What do you mean, 'Is Charlie a man?' No! I know I said he was a 'dead man' but that was just a phrase. He's obviously a boy. There's even a picture of him on the cover of the book!

I take back everything I said earlier. You're every bit as dreadful as the readers of the last book. Possibly worse. I should have learned by now – I only ever get disappointed by readers.

I suggest you run into the bathroom, take a good hard look at yourself in the mirror (if you can bear to) and then repeat three times, 'I'm a massive bum-faced wazzock'.

Meanwhile, I'm going to have to start all over again and I want NO QUESTIONS this time from you people.

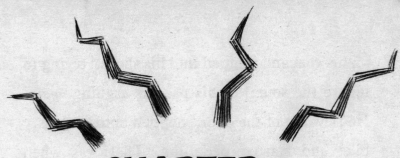

CHAPTER 1

Charlie McGuffin was late again.

And he really couldn't be late this time, or he was a dead[1] man[2].

Charlie had eighteen minutes to get to school if he didn't want to miss the coach which was due to leave at precisely 9 a.m. to take his whole year to the zoo. Miss Fyre, the headmistress, had given them all a warning in assembly the day before: anyone who missed the bus would spend the whole day scrubbing the teachers' toilets with the caretaker, Mr O'Dear.

Charlie hoovered up his corn flakes,[3] flung

[1] Not actually dead.

[2] Not actually a man.

[3] He'd spilled them all over the floor.

on his coat and jumped into his shoes,⁴ trying to ignore the sound of his parents arguing *again*. He flew out of the door,⁵ hopped onto his trusty bike and started pedalling. That was when disaster struck.

His front wheel immediately started making an odd clicking noise and began to deflate. Charlie groaned. He *couldn't* have a puncture.

⁴ This was why he was late – jumping into your shoes is actually very difficult and it took him twenty-seven attempts.

⁵ He didn't really, he just ran. Ordinarily that wouldn't need to be pointed out, but because this is a book about a boy who can change into animals, I thought I should probably be completely clear. Don't worry, it's always very obvious when Charlie's turning into an animal. It's not like he wakes up one morning and BANG! he's a gigantic insect and you're left wondering how on earth that happened. That would be terrible storytelling.

But a puncture it was. Dug deep into the tyre were four drawing pins. *Four?* How had *that* happened? Charlie looked down at the pavement and saw at least twenty more pins scattered all over the ground.

Somebody must have accidentally dropped a box and not picked them up, Charlie thought, without a hint of suspicion, which he really should have had, considering this is the start of the book and suspicious goings-on always happen at the start of books.

Well, that's just really bad luck, Charlie thought. *No one would put drawing pins on the pavement outside my house on purpose.*

Anyway, there was nothing he could do about it now. He was definitely going to be late and miss the school trip. Unless . . .

Unless . . .

Unless I change into an animal, Charlie thought. Then he might JUST have the time to fly to school or run there super-fast, change back into Charlie without being seen AND catch the coach.

Charlie had been changing into animals for several months now, and had learned how to do it whenever he wanted. It was choosing *which* animal that he hadn't quite mastered . . . No matter what he did, it still seemed almost completely random.

Even so, changing was his only chance. It was a risk he had to take.

Charlie dumped his bike underneath a bush in his front garden, and looked around to make sure there was nobody watching.

It looked like the coast was clear.

Charlie closed his eyes and balled his fists, allowing stress to flow into his body. He thought about the rumble of his parents' arguments, which seemed to be non-stop these days. The sound of raised voices and slammed doors gave Charlie a feeling like his lungs were too tight and his stomach had been dropped in icy water. He remembered running upstairs and finding the Great Catsby lying on his bed, out of his box in the kitchen for once, and burying his face in the cat's fur, sobbing.

Charlie recognized the feeling of electricity rippling through his body almost immediately.

He was changing, and changing fast.

Charlie tried imagining the quickest animal he could think of. A great, soaring bird sprang into his brain – a golden eagle with huge wings, designed for maximum speed.

He kept the picture in his mind as the electricity built and built, ripping apart every atom in his body and rebuilding them. He could sense himself shrinking and feel wings sprouting out of his back. But then, to Charlie's dismay, he continued shrinking. Smaller than a golden eagle.

Way smaller.

Maybe I'm going to be a pigeon again, Charlie thought with a groan. *Please – NOT a pigeon. ANYTHING but that!*

No, he realized with relief. *I'm even smaller than a pigeon. A sparrow?*

No, smaller than a sparrow. And anyway, he wasn't growing feathers.

He *had* grown four new legs, some bristly hair and *three*

new eyes on his forehead, but no feathers. His two original eyes had split into thousands of tiny eyes, *and* he'd grown antennae out of his head. Charlie was pretty sure that no bird looked .THAT freaky. He rubbed his two front legs together and buzzed a pair of fragile, transparent wings.

He was tiny now. The size of a –

Charlie was a *fly*.

Ah well, thought Charlie. *It could be worse.* He could still whizz to school super-fast, and while an eagle over the playground would have probably drawn a bit of attention, nobody would notice a boring old house fly, so Charlie reckoned he was pretty safe.

As long as he kept focused and didn't forget who he *really* was, that is. Because, as Charlie had discovered, becoming an animal sometimes made him start to forget that he was actually a human. And that meant trouble . . .

Charlie's antennae twitched and a sudden shiver of nervousness shot through his body. It felt like his body had some sort of tingling fly sixth sense, on high alert to any danger.

With a final rub of his front legs, Charlie buzzed his wings and zipped into the air. He had a curious feeling he was being watched but, despite his many eyes, he couldn't see anybody, so he put it to the back of his tiny fly-mind and started off in the direction of school.

Charlie zoomed happily along, his wings whirring so fast they were a blur. He would never get bored of the feeling of flying – he felt so free, so agile. Plus, his new fly-vision gave him an incredible 360-degree view of the world. It was strange to be flying forward but able to see behind him at the same time. The people and cars below seemed to be moving incredibly slowly. Compared to Charlie, they were crawling in slow-motion. He could see a boy cycling below him who looked like he was pedalling through water.

Suddenly, Charlie's antennae twitched again.

He could smell something *delicious*.

Well, Charlie thought, *I did miss out on my cornflakes. And I'm making such good progress, I reckon I've got time for a quick snack . . .*

Charlie the fly followed the irresistible smell drifting through the air, zig-zagging closer and closer.

Finally, he spotted the source.

There, on the ground.

A scrumptious, exquisite, delicious-looking mound of brown, steaming poo.

Yum, thought Charlie.

Charlie darted down and landed slap-bang on top of it. The intoxicating smell was making his little fly stomach rumble with hunger.

His feet were now covered in poo. He rubbed his two front legs together and then pressed them against his proboscis[6].

Deep down, Charlie knew what he was about to do was wrong.

He knew it was appalling.

He knew it was revolting.

But he just couldn't help it.

Without any warning, Charlie puked on to the pile of poo he was standing on. He watched, proboscis watering, as his puke bubbled and fizzed and turned the poo into a steaming liquid mixture – a sort of poo-and-vomit smoothie. And then he stuck his proboscis into it like a

---

[6] A proboscis is a little tube that flies use to eat. They don't have a mouth or teeth so they can't chew their food, and everything they eat needs to be liquid. And how do they turn their food into liquid? Well, you're about to find out. Warning – it's DISGUSTING.

straw and started to slurp greedily.[7]

Mmmm, thought Charlie. *Yummmm!*

As Charlie was tucking into his foul breakfast, he half-noticed something was approaching him from behind. It looked like a person, but they were moving so slowly it wasn't important. Charlie knew he could fly away at any time.

A bit more lovely, lovely poo smoothie, he thought, *and then I really must get off to school.*

Charlie slurped on until finally his belly was full. It was only as he was wiping the poo from his proboscis that Charlie noticed the danger he was in.

The huge, dark figure was upon him, a vast giant towering unimaginably high. It was swinging something towards him and Charlie tried to jump into the air, wings buzzing furiously.

---

[7] I warned you it was disgusting. But that's what flies do, I'm afraid.

But he'd left it too late.

A huge black box slammed down and swallowed him up.

Charlie sat in the darkness, facing up to his situation.

He was encased in a pitch-black jail, standing on a pile of poo.

Oh no . . .

He'd been *eating* poo!

All sounds from outside the box were muffled but Charlie could hear the unmistakable sound of somebody being sick. And then something slid underneath him and Charlie could no longer feel the warm, squidgy poo under his feet, but hard cardboard instead.

'Ha!' the voice panted between retches. 'I've – ugh, it's all over my hands – I've got you now!'

Charlie had a terrible feeling he recognized the voice.

Panic began to set in and he buzzed inside

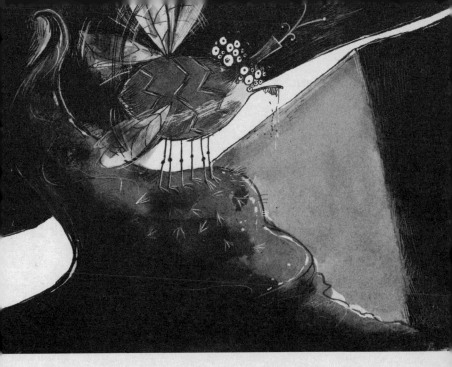

the box, banging against the walls in a desperate attempt to escape.

But it was hopeless. He was completely trapped.

Charlie felt as if he was in a great elevator, being lifted high into the air. If he wasn't mistaken, he was being carried.

'Well, well, well, Charles McGuffin,' said the voice triumphantly. 'Looks like I've finally caught you.'

Charlie *did* know that voice. He'd know it anywhere.

'I told you I'd get you, one of these days,' gloated the voice. 'And you flew right into my trap. Now when you change back, I'm going to make sure the whole world sees what a freak you are!'

With sickening dread, Charlie realized he'd been captured by Dylan van der Gruyne.

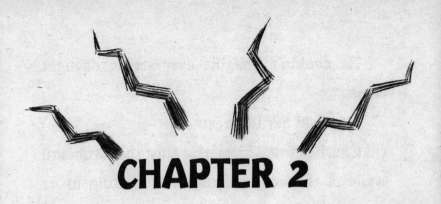

CHAPTER 2

Charlie the fly sat in total darkness, his tiny heart thrumming in panic. He tried to calm himself down and figure out what to do. His cardboard prison was bumping up and down, and Charlie guessed by the steady rhythm that he was in Dylan's pocket, and that Dylan was walking.

Charlie was well and truly stuck.

He had to change back – and fast.

But Charlie needed to be calm in order to change, and there was no escape from his spiralling thoughts.

He felt as if he was trapped in a coffin, buried deep under the earth.

He couldn't imagine ever seeing daylight again.

He could hardly breathe.

Charlie hurled himself against the cardboard walls of the box, banging and bashing to no avail, until he finally gave up and miserably clung to one of the sides. He couldn't even tell if he was the right way up.

Slowly but surely, Charlie the fly felt himself start separating from Charlie the boy. Bit by bit, he could feel his thoughts and memories slipping away, and Charlie knew they would go on shrinking until they disappeared altogether, and all that would be left would be a fly in a matchbox.

Charlie fought the terror that clutched at him.

He tried to slow his breathing and remember all the people who loved him: his mum and dad; his brother, SmoothMove; his best friends,

Mohsen and Wogan, and of course, Flora. He clung to warm memories of them, desperately trying to stop himself sinking into the dreadful quicksand of forgetfulness that threatened to engulf him.

Slowly, the slide into oblivion stopped, and Charlie found he could still remember who he was. He might be a fly with a pooey proboscis, but he was *Charlie* the fly.

He was still stuck, though. The happy memories had been enough to stop him losing himself, but hadn't been quite enough to get him to change back.

Through the cardboard, he could hear faint noises from outside.

It sounded like he was in a playground. Dylan must have reached school, and Charlie was still stuck in his pocket.

'Come on, Van der Gruyne!' shouted the unmistakable voice of Mr Wind, the Head of

Year. 'You nearly missed the bus, boy. Get on quickly!'

Charlie felt the bumping steps as Dylan clambered on to the bus.

'Now,' Mr Wind continued, 'that's everybody ... apart from McGuffin. Anybody seen Charles McGuffin? No? Well, he was warned! Hope he has fun on bog-duty with Mr O'Dear! Driver, if you will, to the zoo!'

Through his six sticky feet, Charlie felt the vibration of the bus engine starting, then a sudden bump as Dylan sat down.

Now Charlie was REALLY stuck. There was no way he could change back now. Everyone would see him.

As the bus drove further away from the school, the babbling of the children became louder and more excitable.

But above the chatter, Charlie could clearly hear two voices arguing.

'He does!'

'He *doesn't*!'

'He DOES!'

'He **DOES NOT!**'

Charlie would know them anywhere. It was Mohsen and Wogan.

'How do you know? You haven't even seen it!'

'Right, Flora, can you settle this?' That was

Mohsen speaking, Charlie thought, smiling inside. 'Does Spider-Man blow webs out of his bum?'

'Does Spider-Man blow webs out of his bum?!' That was Flora's voice, and Charlie's heart leaped with joy. He could imagine the look of disbelief in her face. 'Is that what you're really asking me?'

'He does!' exclaimed Wogan. 'In the first movie – the one with the evil sheep! Spider-Man bends over and blasts webs out like massive farts all over them!'

Charlie felt laughter begin to ripple through him like sunshine on water.

'Wogan,' Flora said wearily. 'Please. Listen to yourself. Spider-Man blasting webs out of his bum on to *evil sheep*? Are you sure this wasn't a dream?'

'Ah,' Wogan replied. 'Yes. Now you mention it, there's actually a strong possibility it was a dream. In fact, come to think of it, I'm almost certain it *was* a dream.'

If Charlie hadn't been a fly at that moment, he would have roared with laughter. But as he *was* a fly, he just hung upside down, laughing silently to himself.

And that was all it took to make Charlie start changing back: happiness and laughter and love.

For the first time he could remember, Charlie didn't *want* to change back – he was on a bus packed with his classmates! – but he couldn't stop himself. The image of Spider-Man bending over and shooting a web out of his bum on to evil sheep was just too funny, and Charlie felt himself starting to grow . . .

Dylan could feel it too, and grabbed at his pocket, but it was too late.

'Noooooo!' he cried.

With a gigantic ripping sound, Charlie smashed out of the matchbox, burst out of

Dylan's trousers. And a moment later, he had changed completely back to human-Charlie, and was sitting on Dylan's lap in the back corner seat of the bus.

'Charlie!' called Wogan, spotting him. 'There you are! Where've you been?'

'We thought you missed the bus!' said Mohsen. 'But why are you sitting on Dylan's knee? There are plenty of seats.'

'They must have finally got over that whole

"mortal enemies" thing,' said Wogan.

'Well isn't that wonderful,' Mohsen beamed. 'Everybody's friends now, sitting on each other's knees.'

'I knew you two would put your differences aside eventually,' said Flora. 'I'm so proud of you both.'

'We have NOT put our differences aside,' said Dylan, shoving Charlie off his lap. 'And we are STILL mortal enemies!'

'Ah well,' said Wogan. 'Never mind. I thought it was too good to be true.'

'And not only will I wreak a terrible revenge on you, McGuffin,' continued Dylan. 'But you owe me a new pair of trousers as well.'

Dylan stormed off to the front of the bus, clutching the hole in his trousers so he didn't show the whole bus his pants.

'Will that boy ever change – hang on, what's that?' Wogan asked, pointing at Charlie.

'What's what?' Charlie asked.

'That! All over your face,' said Wogan, still pointing.

'Ugh,' said Mohsen. 'It's like brown stuff all round your mouth and nose.'

Charlie knew *exactly* what it was.

Poo smoothie.

'I *reeeeeally* hope it's chocolate,' Mohsen continued.

'It's nothing!' said Charlie, as brightly as

possible. 'Anyway! Let's move on.'

'It's not *nothing*!' Wogan continued. 'It's definitely *something*. Something crusty and, hang on, can anyone smell –'

'IT'S NOTHING!' Charlie shouted, the look of thunder in his eyes daring someone to say anything more on the matter.

Nobody dared say any more on the matter.

'Now does anybody have a wet wipe?'

***

Mr Wind and Miss Fyre (who always took school trips together because of their 'synergy, shared values and compatible work ethic') got off the coach first, followed by the class, who piled off in an excitable crush. As Charlie clambered down the steps, Miss Fyre caught sight of him.

'There you are, McGuffin! Mr Wind, I thought you said he was absent?'

Mr Wind looked flustered.

'But . . . he was!' He turned to Charlie. 'How did you get here? You weren't on the coach!'

'Well, I was, sir,' replied Charlie. 'You just saw me get off.'

'Don't be cheeky in front of Miss Fyre, boy. She doesn't like cheek, do you, darli– I mean, Miss Fyre?'

'Not one bit, Mr Wind!'

'Well, you're here now, McGuffin, and I've got my eye on you. Pay attention, everyone!' Mr Wind shouted, now addressing the whole of the bus. 'I want you all back on the coach by 3 p.m. or I'll tell the zookeepers to feed you to the alligators!'

The children separated into small groups as they headed inside the zoo.

Miss Fyre had managed to use her emergency stapler to staple Dylan's trousers together, but you could still see flashes of his Incredible Hulk underpants as he stormed off. Charlie was walking next to Wogan, Flora and Mohsen. Behind them, in a close huddle were Daisy and a small girl with glasses and long blonde hair called Lola Coaster.

They were muttering secretively, shooting furtive glances towards the boys.

Charlie guessed what they were talking about. There was only one topic of conversation at the moment that was causing groups of girls to huddle together, muttering secretively and shooting furtive glances at groups of terrified boys.

The School Dance.

It was almost the end of term, and who was going to the dance with whom was a matter of fierce debate. And although Charlie was dreading it because he *really* couldn't dance and didn't know who he was going to go with, he couldn't help but be caught up in the excitement.

'They're huddling, aren't they?' asked Wogan.

Mohsen nodded. 'AND shooting furtive glances!'

Wogan looked worried. 'Can you see what they're saying? Are they talking about the dance?'

Flora rolled her eyes. 'Oh, who cares about

the silly dance! It's all anybody is talking about!'

'Do you think I should ask Daisy?' asked Wogan, ignoring Flora. 'Oh, this is a nightmare. This is worse than that boat trip where I felt so sick that I accidentally puked on Mohsen's head.'

'I hate to disagree with you there, old friend,' said Mohsen. 'But I'm absolutely certain this is *not* worse than when you puked on my head.'

'Look, guys,' said Charlie. 'I suggest we forget all about the dance for today, OK? Let's just enjoy the zoo. So – which animals should we go to first? The penguins?'

'No!' said Wogan. 'I *hate* penguins.'

'What do you have against penguins?' asked Charlie, surprised.

'I don't trust them,' said Wogan. 'Greasy-looking birds that can't even fly and live in the sea? No, thanks.'

'Right,' said Charlie. 'No penguins then. Lions? Tigers? Goril–'

'Chinchillas!' interrupted Wogan.

'Pardon?' replied Charlie, staring at Wogan.

'There are chinchillas at the petting zoo. We should definitely go there first.'

'OK . . .' said Charlie. 'If you really want, I guess?'

'It's Daisy,' explained Mohsen, matter-of-factly. 'She is going through a chinchilla phase.'

'That's just a coincidence!' exclaimed a red-faced Wogan. 'I just like the way chinchillas are . . . are . . . so slippery? And . . . scaly?'

Flora gave Wogan a pointed look. 'Wogan. Do you even know what a chinchilla is?'

'Oh, you're going to see the chinchillas?'

It was Daisy. The girls had caught the boys up without them noticing.

'Yes,' replied Mohsen. 'Chinchillas have for a long time been Wogan's favourite animal,' he said, giving Wogan a not-so-subtle wink. 'So we are going to the petting zoo to pet the chinchillas.

Which are small and furry, Wogan.'

'I knew that!' said Wogan, looking mortified.

'Oh!' said Daisy. 'I used to like chinchillas. But I'm not into them any more. I like chameleons now. So we're off to see the reptiles. Bye!'

Daisy gave a little wave and Lola added a nervous smile, which seemed to be pointed in the direction of Mohsen. Then the girls linked arms and walked off in the opposite direction.

Wogan turned to Mohsen, a look of fury on his face. 'Thanks a BUNCH, Mohsen!'

'What?!'

'You made me look like a right lemon in front of Daisy!'

'Look, Wogan. You've got to relax,' said Mohsen, putting a fatherly arm round Wogan. 'You need to forget about Daisy. Put her out of your mind. Now – does anybody reckon Lola smiled at me? I think she did. What does that

mean? Do you think she's going to ask me to the school dance?'

Flora rolled her eyes again. As she did, they spotted the petting zoo just a few metres away.

'Come on,' she said. 'Let's take a look.'

***

They traipsed inside but there was no sign of chinchillas. Instead, beside an empty cage, there was a laminated sign, which said:

!!!!HELP!!!!

OUR CHINCHILLAS ARE MISSING!

ANY INFORMATION LEADING TO THE RETURN
OF THE CHINCHILLAS WILL BE REWARDED

PLEASE SPEAK TO A ZOOKEEPER IF U KNOW
ANYTHING AT ALL. ABOUT THE WHEREABOUTS
OF THE CHINCHILLAS, I MEAN.

WARNING: DO NOT APPROACH THE CHINCHILLAS!
THEY ARE DANGEROUSLY ADORABLE AND YOU
WILL FALL IN LOVE WITH THEM IMMEDIATELY.

BUT PLEASE DON'T WORRY! WE ARE SURE THE
CHINCHILLAS ARE **ABSOLUTELY FINE** AND
TOTALLY HAVEN'T BEEN EATEN, EVEN THOUGH
THERE WERE LITTLE BITS OF FUR AND STUFF
ROUND THE CAGE.

'Well, that's a shame,' said Flora. 'I was looking forward to petting some chinchillas after all that.'

'Never mind!' said Wogan, brightly. 'How about we go and see the chameleons instead?'

The gang shrugged and started walking slowly in the direction of the Reptile House.

***

After much plodding round the zoo, looking at animals and observing the strange habits of all the different species and definitely NOT just following Daisy and Lola, it was time for a packed lunch.[8] That was followed by even more plodding round the zoo, looking at animals and observing the strange habits of Daisy and Lola.

---

[8] For those wondering, Mohsen had a new sandwich box. For those who haven't read *Charlie Turns Into a T-Rex*, Mohsen had a new sandwich box because Wogan did a wee in the last one and Charlie ended up swimming in the wee. Now if THAT doesn't encourage you to go back and read the book then NOTHING will.

Well into the afternoon, the four friends found themselves at the lion enclosure. There, throwing stones over the fence at the mournful-looking lions, was Dylan.

'Look at him,' said Flora. 'What a horrible thing to do. Someone really needs to teach him a lesson.'

And that gave Charlie an idea.

A very naughty idea.

And naughty ideas are always the best ideas. Unless you're a policeman. Or the prime minister. Or the Pope.

'You know what, Flora,' Charlie said, with a wink. 'That's exactly what I'm going to do. I'm going to teach him not to mess with lions. Or *me*!'

Flora frowned. 'What does that wink mean? What are you planning, Charlie?'

'Oh, just a little surprise for Dylan . . .'

'Charlie. Do NOT get yourself in trouble, OK?'

'Flora, in the last few months you have convinced me to break into Miss Fyre's office AND the headquarters of Van der Gruyne Industries. At least I'm not doing anything against the law this time. And anyway, what good is having a superpower if you can't use it against a villain every now and again . . . ?'

And with that foolproof slice of logic, Charlie ran off behind a small low building with a sign outside, which read:

THE MAGICAL PALACE OF STICK INSECTS

ENJOY A WORLD OF FUN TRYING TO SPOT THESE ENTHRALLING TWIG-LIKE CREATURES AMONGST LOTS AND LOTS OF TWIGS!

P.S. If you see one, can you INFORM A MEMBER OF STAFF because we're NOT SURE if there actually ARE any . . .

Charlie hid deep in some overgrown bushes, closed his eyes and breathed in deeply. He pinpointed the direct centre of his fears: it wasn't actually the arguments between his mum and dad – it was the long, cold silences in between. Like when he'd heard his father shout, 'Oh, what's the point any more?' and his mother had shouted in reply, 'Maybe there IS no point!' – and they hadn't talked for hours afterwards. It was *those* silences that scared Charlie the most.

In Charlie breathed, facing up to the feeling that was always in his stomach, sometimes forgotten when he was having fun with his friends, but always churning away in the background. In he breathed, accepting the bad in his life, but turning it around inside himself, transforming it into power.

As Charlie felt tears prickling behind his closed eyes, he sensed the change start, the electricity spark and fizz through him, his atoms rearranging themselves.

And Charlie's mind was filled with two things: a picture of a fierce lion and revenge.

Revenge on Dylan, who wanted to harm him and his friends.

Maybe *that* would help get rid of the feeling in his stomach.

Anger seared through Charlie. He could feel his teeth and claws growing, sharpening.

He'd done it! It was working! He was changing into a lion!

Charlie could feel great, green leathery scales forming on his skin.

OK, maybe it *wasn't* working, then.

He wasn't changing into a lion. Despite practising in his bedroom whenever

he could, Charlie still couldn't get the hang of changing into the animals he wanted.

So what *was* he changing into?

He flopped on to the ground, his body growing incredibly long, his arms transforming into stumpy legs with lethal-looking claws.

His face lengthened into a wide snout and powerful jaw.

A great tail grew out of his behind. He swished it in a wide arc, crushing bushes, and snapped his jaws together.

Maybe he wasn't a lion, but this would do. This would *absolutely* do.

Charlie pushed his colossal body forward with his claws, scooping up great mounds of earth as he went.

He came out from behind the Magical Palace of Stick Insects and swung his massive head, one way then the next, sniffing the air.

He could smell Dylan, and he started moving his great body in that direction.

A plump lady with two small pugs on leads turned a corner and caught sight of

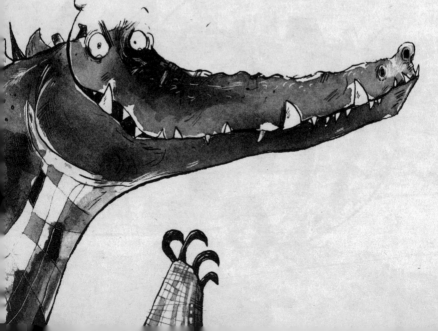

Charlie. For a moment she froze, staring. And then she unfroze and screamed at the top of her lungs:

'AN ALLIGATOR! THERE'S AN ESCAPED ALLIGATOR!'

The lady turned and fled in the opposite direction, her dogs scampering as fast as they could ahead of her, yapping in terror.

No, no, no, Charlie thought, a wicked gleam in his cold green eye. *Not an alligator.*

A crocodile.[9]

---

[9] Charlie was correct. He was a crocodile. But not just any crocodile. He was a saltwater crocodile. He was six metres long – longer than a car and half the weight of one. He was the largest reptile on the planet, with a powerful jaw lined with ten-centimetre-long teeth, and a lethal tail and claws. Crocodiles haven't evolved in ten million years because they are the perfect killing machine. And that perfect killing machine was heading Dylan's way.

CHAPTER 3

The scent of Dylan on the wind was irresistible.

Charlie the crocodile charged down the path, past his gobsmacked friends, following the smell.

Whenever a member of the public strayed into his path, they turned tail and fled, usually screaming. Which is entirely understandable and exactly what you should do if you are unfortunate enough to come across a crocodile, or an alligator for that matter.

Charlie wasn't bothered though. He had one target on his mind.

There was Dylan, now so busy taunting some monkeys that he didn't notice the screams of terror from the people around him . . . Or the six-metre crocodile sneaking up behind him.

It was only when the monkeys started whooping that Dylan began to suspect that there was something unusual going on.

'Are those monkeys . . . laughing?' Dylan asked the woman standing next to him, frozen in terror as she stared at the crocodile. 'Look at them. They're finding *something* funny. That one's rolling on the floor!'

The woman made a terrified little honking noise.

'Hang about . . . now they're pointing,' said Dylan. 'What's that about?'

Slowly, Dylan turned round.

And there behind him, jaws slavering and teeth glistening, ready to pounce, was Charlie the crocodile.

Dylan let out a small mew of terror. And then ran.

Charlie gave chase.

When he had started the hunt, Charlie's plan had just been to terrify Dylan, but now all the anger he felt for the misery Dylan had caused him and his friends came together as one thought: *bite him.*

Chomp him.

Crunch his bones and tear his flesh.

Despite Dylan's head start, Charlie was gaining on him. He **snapped** his jaws – but caught only thin air.

He realized what he was doing was wrong and knew deep down he shouldn't eat Dylan, but the instinct was impossible to resist. Dylan *deserved* it.

SNAP!

Again, Charlie's great jaws slammed shut, and this time he caught the back of Dylan's hastily-stapled trousers, and ripped them open again. Dylan kept running in sheer panic, trying to hold up what was left of his trousers and underpants AND hide his bum at the same time.

That was impossible though and, as Dylan ran, his trousers dropped completely down, got tangled up in his feet and he fell forward onto his face, displaying his bare bum to the world.

But worse than that, the crocodile was upon him.

Charlie gave a hiss of victory, and shook his head to get rid of the shredded Incredible Hulk underpants which hung off his front teeth. He crawled forward and placed a heavy claw on Dylan's back, rolling him over like a rag doll.

No, Charlie thought. *I can't do this!*

Yes, you can, the crocodile part of him thought. *The world is a cruel place and people just need to realize that.*

Dylan whimpered with dread as the crocodile crawled forward until its head was level with his. It eyed him, and the cold black slit in the

green orb narrowed as it got closer and closer. Dylan felt hot, foul breath on his face as the crocodile opened its vast jaws. He closed his eyes and waited for the bite that would end his young life.

'Stop!'

Charlie turned his great head to see who had interrupted his dinner.

It was Mr Wind, and he was charging towards Charlie, brandishing a broom high above his head like a sword, with Miss Fyre in quick pursuit.

'Stop!' cried Mr Wind again. 'Get away from that bare-bummed boy!'

Charlie snapped out of his trance and realized what he was about to do. He had been about to eat Dylan!

Mr Wind reached Charlie and started hitting him with the broom.

Charlie tried hissing a warning but Mr Wind, emboldened by Miss Fyre's shouts of encouragement, kept whacking him again and again.

Charlie began backing away, and Dylan took his chance, scrabbling off on all fours and not caring who could see his bum.

At the same moment, something landed round Charlie's neck. It was some sort of lasso attached to a stick, held by a beefy-looking zookeeper with a huge moustache.

The more Charlie tried to free himself, the tighter the lasso became.

'Come on, you!' the zookeeper said, tugging Charlie forward. 'Let's get you back where you belong! Lord alone knows how you escaped.'

Charlie was stuck. He had no choice but to be led along the path like a dog on a leash. They soon reached a small door in a wall, like a giant cat flap, which the zookeeper opened.

'Back in there with you!' The zookeeper manoeuvred Charlie skilfully through the flap and into a tunnel. When he was in, the leash round his neck was released and the flap snapped shut behind him.

Charlie couldn't help laughing – the memory of Dylan running away in terror, with his pants hanging off him and his bum poking out, was just too funny. And as the laughter rippled through Charlie, he began to change. His tail was already disappearing, his skin becoming smoother, his body shrinking. A moment later, Charlie the crocodile was no more. He was back to plain old Charlie.

Still chortling to himself, he looked at his new predicament. He was stuck in the short tunnel, and the flap behind him had been locked by the zookeeper. He had to keep on going forward. In front of him was another flap and Charlie stopped chortling as he began to get a sneaking feeling he knew what lay on the other side.

But Charlie had no choice. He pushed his way through and crawled out into a large grassy slope dotted with trees.

At the bottom of the slope was a huge pond, fringed by tall reeds.

And surrounding the pond, staring at Charlie, were half a dozen huge and very menacing reptiles.

Charlie was in the crocodile enclosure.

They turned as one and stared at the newcomer who had suddenly appeared in their territory.

Then three of the crocodiles started lumbering towards him.

Charlie had never, ever been so terrified in his life.

The crocodiles lashed their tails eagerly.

They knew *exactly* what to do with a small boy trapped in their enclosure.

And it wasn't play table tennis with him.

It was dinner time and their jaws were drooling at the sudden meal that had presented itself to them.

Charlie knew he was finished if he did nothing and just waited for help – he had to get out. He saw only one hope, one sliver of a chance. Without a second's thought, he started running *towards* the crocodiles.

The beasts' jaws were wide open in shock at the sight of their dinner hurtling towards them.

Charlie ran as fast as he could and, at the last moment, he jumped over the snapping teeth on to the nearest crocodile's head.

He bounced off, straight on to another croc's head.

He trampolined off that one too, hop-scotching straight on to a third.

Then, with a great leap off the last crocodile's

head, jaws chomping wildly underneath him, Charlie scrambled up the wall of the enclosure, grabbed on to the edge and pulled himself over, to the gasps of the crowd gathered outside and furious hisses from the crocodiles below.

AUTHOR'S NOTE

I hate to interrupt the story but I have sorry news to announce – I am afraid I've had to sack the illustrator of this book, Sarah Horne.

I'm sure you will agree that Sarah Horne's pictures have been adequate, but I'm sorry to report she has been getting a little too big for her boots. Since our association began, I have paid her the wages we agreed: two pounds fifty per day and all the cold rice she can eat. I even occasionally treated her to a banana, if I found one too bruised and blackened for my taste. This was not in her contract – I did it out of the simple generosity that comes naturally to me.

But this was not good enough for Sarah Horne.

She has complained endlessly, and repeatedly claimed she 'feels constantly weak with hunger'.

Intolerable.

The final straw came when I discovered she had been inserting hidden messages into the illustrations of this book. If you look carefully at page 31, you will see what I mean. Deeply rude and immature.

Understandably, I have reached the end of my tether and have sacked her with immediate effect.

I'm sure you all agree that drawing *pictures* doesn't take any particular skill, so I have decided that from this point on, I shall do them myself.

Here are some examples of pictures of the main characters from this book, drawn by me. While the most eagle-eyed of you might spot some *tiny* differences from the previous illustrations, to most readers the changes will be unnoticeable, and certainly won't affect your enjoyment of the book at all.

Charlie

Dylan

A goat

A bee

A swan

A rabbit

An octopus

Charlie turned into a T-Rex

CHAPTER 4

By the time Charlie made it back to the coach, some of the chaos had died down.

'Here he is!' Miss Fyre called into the coach when she caught sight of Charlie tramping across the car park.

Coach

Charlie

'Where on earth have you been?' Miss Fyre snapped. 'You're lucky we didn't leave you here! We were due to set off ages ago.'

AUTHOR'S NOTE II

I apologize for interrupting this story once again.

According to the publisher of this book, my pictures 'lack any artistic merit' and are 'frankly more than a little disturbing'.

If you recall, this is *exactly* what they said about the famous artist Van Gogh.

The 'publisher' continued by insisting I apologize publicly to the 'illustrator' Sarah Horne and give the job back to her – together with a pay rise – or they will not publish this book.

So:

Dear Sarah,

I'm soooooo sorry I was rude about your pictures. You are sooooooo super-talented. Honestly.

I hope you enjoy your pay-rise to three pounds fifty a day.

Yours,
Sam Copeland
The Writer (the one with the actual talent)

P.S. Don't think you'll be getting any more free bananas.

Anyway. Back to the story.

CHAPTER 4
(again)

By the time Charlie made it back to the coach, some of the chaos had died down.

'Here he is!' Miss Fyre called into the coach when she caught sight of Charlie tramping across the car park.

'Where on earth have you been?' Miss Fyre snapped. 'You're lucky we didn't leave you here! We were due to set off ages ago.'

Charlie grimaced. In no way did he think he was lucky.

Mr Wind was sitting on the front passenger seat, wrapped in a silver foil blanket. Miss Fyre was massaging his temples to help him with the shock.

Charlie walked down the now-moving coach and saw Dylan. He was staring out the window, pale-faced and trembling ever so slightly, but when he caught sight of Charlie, he glared at him.

'I know it was you!' Dylan whispered, in a voice dripping with fury.

'What?' said Charlie innocently.

'Oh, don't even try to pretend! YOU were the crocodile! It was YOU who tried to eat me.'

'I don't know what you're talking about,' said Charlie.

'Fine! Play it that way. But don't think you've got the better of me, McGuffin. I've already started a plan to destroy you and there's nothing you can do about it. You'll regret the day we ever crossed paths.'

'Dylan, I already regret the day we crossed paths,' sighed Charlie.

'Very funny. Well, you won't be laughing for long.'

'I'm sure I – hang on. What's that you're wearing?'

'It's a skirt, McGuffin, OK? My trousers got ripped, as you know full well, and there were no spare trousers. So I'm wearing a skirt. And mark my words, this skirt isn't going to improve relations between us. On the contrary. I'm going

to ruin you because of this skirt. Destroy you. I'm every nightmare you've ever had. I'm your worst dream come true. I'm everything you've ever been afraid of.'

'Dylan, have you been watching horror movies again? Seriously, you should stop.'

'Get out of my sight.'

Charlie left Dylan stewing in his skirt, and saw Mohsen waving to him from the back seat. As he bounced down the coach, all he could hear was excitable chatter about the escaped crocodile.

Charlie flumped down in between Wogan and Mohsen, who listened in wide-eyed silence as Charlie told them of his escape from the crocodile compound.

'Holy rollers, that is AWESOME,' said Mohsen.

'That really is awesome, Charlie. That is nearly as awesome as when Mohsen got the whistle stuck up his nose.'

'That actually really wasn't that awesome,' replied Mohsen. 'My left nostril whistled for days and I had to go to hospital to get it removed. In fact, that was one of your worst ideas, Wogan. Charlie nearly getting eaten by crocodiles is way more awes–'

Flora, who was sitting in front of them and had been listening the whole time, suddenly swung around.

'No! What Charlie did was NOT awesome! It was dangerous and stupid.' She fixed her eyes on Charlie. 'You let your anger get the better of you. You could have been eaten by crocodiles, just because you wanted to give Dylan a scare. That's . . . just . . . so . . . NOT AWESOME! In fact, it's the LEAST AWESOME thing I have ever seen anybody do!'

'Steady on, Flora,' said Wogan bravely. 'Don't say that.'

'I WILL say that. And Charlie – tell me!

Were you really just giving Dylan a scare, or did you end up trying to eat him? Because that's what it looked like.'

Charlie looked at his feet, shame-faced. Flora was right. It had been a silly risk. And he *had* nearly eaten Dylan. And why had he done it?

Flora was right again; he was angry.

Angry and scared.

Angry and scared about the silences between his mum and dad that seemed to stretch on forever, the words in between like ice, cold and brittle.

★★★

By the time the coach arrived back at the school, there was already a crowd of journalists waiting.[10] They swarmed around the new school

---

[10] How the journalists had got to the school so quickly, no one would ever know. Although if you were to check Mr Wind's mobile phone records, you would see the last numbers dialled were the *Telegraph*, *The Times*, the *Mail*, the *Sun* and the *Mirror*. Just a coincidence, I'm sure.

chicken coop, chickens clucking contentedly in the background, cameras slung round their necks.[11] As the children all piled off the bus, the journalists started shouting and snapping photos.

Centre of attention was, of course, Mr Wind, still wrapped in his silver blanket like an earthquake victim, who waved bravely as he disembarked the coach, slowly. Very slowly.

'Can you give us a comment, Mr Wind?' one journalist shouted.

'Are you a hero, Mr Wind?'

'Did you fight the crocodile single-handedly, Mr Wind?'

'Mr Wind, what exactly is your relationship with –'

'That's quite enough, ladies and gentlemen!' shouted Miss Fyre, using her sternest teacher voice.

---

[11] The journalists' necks, not the chickens'.

The journalists fell silent like naughty schoolchildren.

'I shall now read you a brief statement on behalf of Mr Wind!' Miss Fyre continued, raising a hastily scrawled note. '"While on a field trip to the local zoo, one of our pupils was approached by an escaped crocodile. I immediately recognized the risk that the crocodile was going to attack him or, worse, might have gone on to attack somebody important, such as Miss Fyre. I then merely acted as any *extremely* brave member of the public would do. Without a single thought for my own safety, I jumped on the crocodile and repeatedly hit it with a broom. Through my strength and cunning, I was able to single-handedly defeat the deadly crocodile in mortal combat. Others might consider my actions to be heroic and wish to start a campaign for me to receive some sort of an award for outstanding bravery in the face of terrible danger. But that is not for me to say. I do not consider myself a hero. Thank you.'"

Miss Fyre carefully folded the statement away.

'Now, Mr Wind might not consider himself a hero, but I do. However, I must ask you to respect his privacy. Any requests for interviews or features or full-page photographs of Mr Wind and myself should be sent to my personal email address.'

As Miss Fyre began handing out business cards to the journalists, Charlie and his friends began walking quietly home. They had hardly started, though, when Lola suddenly appeared next to them, with Daisy trailing a few metres behind.

'Hi, guys!' Lola said brightly.

'Hi,' the friends replied sullenly.

'So, Wogan,' Lola said. 'Daisy was wondering if you'd go to the school dance with her?'

'Errr . . . yes,' replied Wogan, in shock, a nervous smile edging on to his face. 'OK then.'

'Great!' Lola scampered back to join Daisy.

'Did that just happen?' asked Wogan.

'It sure did, my friend,' said Mohsen, clapping Wogan on the back.

'Wow,' said Wogan. 'Wow.'

Flora let out a big huff. 'I mean, who even cares about who you go to the silly dance with?'

For some reason, Charlie found that he did care, and he didn't reply.

Flora and Charlie were lost in their own silences until suddenly Flora stopped.

'Hang on a minute,' she said. 'Look at that.'

She pointed at a sign pinned to a tree:

LOST!

HAVE YOU SEEN OUR MUCH-LOVED FAMILY DOG?
HE IS CALLED BUTCH AND HAS BEEN MISSING
FOR TWO DAYS.

PLEASE CALL 07958 43677

REWARD OFFERED!

P.S. Has anyone also lost a lion or tiger?
Very large feline paw prints were found
in our garden the day Butch went missing.
We're sure that's a total coincidence, though.

'So? What's your point, Flor?' asked Wogan.

'I mean, it's very sad and all that, but . . .'

'Just follow me,' said Flora.

She ran to a nearby lamp-post and pointed again.

MISSING!

HAVE YOU SEEN OUR CAT MR SOCKS?

HE IS EXTREMELY VICIOUS AND WEES
ALL OVER THE HOUSE, SO WHY ANYBODY
WOULD STEAL HIM IS BEYOND US.

IF YOU FIND HIM,
PLEASE KEEP HIM.

MR SOCKS SCARES US.

'Strange, isn't it?' Flora said.

'It's just some missing pets,' said Charlie.

'Maybe you're right. I'm sure it's just a coincidence,' Flora replied, and smiled at Charlie.

Charlie smiled back. He might not understand Flora, but he was very glad they were back to being friends again.

Charlie's good mood didn't last long though. The minute he walked through the front door he knew something wasn't right. Even though everybody was home, the air was thick with silence.

He could tell he'd walked straight into another argument between his mum and dad.

'We are just going round and round in circles!' Charlie heard his mum shout. 'It's pointless!'

'Well if it's so pointless –' Charlie's dad shouted, before Charlie slammed the front door and the shouting stopped immediately.

His dad, red in the face, stormed out of the

kitchen, ruffled Charlie's hair as he went past and gave him an apologetic smile.

Charlie went into the kitchen and his mum was sat at the table, wiping her eyes with a tea towel. When she saw Charlie, she quickly jumped up and went to the sink, and began washing some dishes.

'Hello, love,' she said, with forced brightness. 'How was your day?'

Words spilled out of Charlie as he gabbled the story, hoping the remarkable events of the day would put a smile back on his mum's face.

'And then,' Charlie finished, 'there was an escaped crocodile and it nearly ate Dylan and it was right on top of him but then Mr Wind came along with a broom and hit it until the crocodile had to get off Dylan and I – I mean *it* – had to run away.'

When he reached the end of the story, his mum gave him a curious look.

'What an extraordinary story, Charlie. Is that all there is to it?'

'What do you mean?' asked Charlie.

'Is there something else you want to tell me? You can tell me anything, you know. You won't be in trouble.'

Charlie was annoyed. She must suspect him of having something to do with the escaped crocodile.

'What do you think I did? Let a crocodile loose? You always think I'm up to something bad!' Charlie was surprised at the force of his anger. 'And maybe there's something *you're* not telling *me*! Like why you and Dad are shouting all the time! It's horrible!'

Charlie's mum looked at him for a long moment without saying anything. Charlie saw she had tears in her eyes and that did nothing to make him feel any better.

'You're right,' she said, finally. 'Go and call your brother and your dad in, will you?'

Charlie swallowed, his mouth dry and his heart fluttering, but he did as he was told.

SmoothMove and Charlie's dad came in and sat at the table. Charlie didn't want to sit down. Although he had started it, he suddenly found he really didn't want this conversation to happen.

'I think it's time to tell them,' said Charlie's mum.

His dad nodded, and tried to say something, but the words wouldn't come out.

'Tell us what?' asked SmoothMove in a small voice.

'I'm so, so sorry, boys,' Charlie's mum said, as tears started trickling down her face.

And then Charlie's whole world fell apart.

***

'Oh, Charlie, I'm so, so sorry,' said Flora.

'Funny, that's exactly what my mum said,' Charlie replied, not smiling.

Charlie had called an emergency meeting at Mohsen's house with Wogan, Mohsen and Flora. The bombshell his parents had dropped was still swirling round his mind.

'Your mum and I have been having difficulties for some time,' his dad had said. 'And it's not fair on you guys, being around us when we're arguing all the time.'

Charlie had felt his knees go weak. He sat down. He'd known what was coming next.

'So,' his mum had said. 'We've decided it's best if your father and I separate. Just for a trial period.'

Charlie's stomach had felt like he'd just gone over the top of a roller coaster. He couldn't believe what he was hearing. He wanted to unhear it.

His parents had talked for much longer after that – about how it wasn't anyone's fault, about how they loved Charlie and SmoothMove just as much as always – but the words had all jumbled in Charlie's mind. Then SmoothMove started shouting, and his mum and dad started crying, and Charlie had just sat there feeling tiny.

And he still felt tiny now, even surrounded by his friends.

'Yeah, that's just rubbish,' said Wogan.

'Well, you know we're here for you, Charlie,' said Mohsen.

'Thanks, guys,' said Charlie, glumly.

'But loads of parents get separated,' continued Mohsen. 'Like there's maybe four kids in our class whose parents have split up. Lola's aren't together.'

'Yeah, and Lucy K and Lucy M – both have parents that have separated. It happens all the time,' Wogan chipped in.

'I know,' said Charlie. 'It's just that this bad stuff always happens to me. First my brother got ill, then we nearly lost the house, and now this. It's not fair. I just want to have to worry about *normal* stuff, like the big spelling test tomorrow and the school dance.'

'You're right, Charlie. It is totally unfair,' said Flora. 'And it's fine for you to feel worried. The best thing you can do is just to try and accept that rubbish stuff happens and sometimes there's nothing you can do about it.'

'Yeah,' said Charlie. 'It's just really diff–'

'Hang on. WAIT A MINUTE. There's a big spelling test tomorrow?!' Wogan looked pale. 'As in *tomorrow* tomorrow?'

'Yes,' said Mohsen. 'The really important spelling test that we're in huge trouble if we fail. Remember?'

'Oh no!' Wogan wailed. 'I totally forgot! I haven't learned them! I'm in SO MUCH trouble. This is the WORST thing that has EVER happened to ANYBODY.'

'Wogan,' said Flora, with dangerous calm. 'Charlie has just told us that his parents are separating.'

'Yes, but –'

'AND YOU SIT THERE COMPLAINING ABOUT YOUR SPELLING TEST!' Flora blasted.

'Ah. Yes. I see,' said Wogan. 'Sorry about that, Charlie. Your parents separating is a bit worse than a spelling test, definitely.'

'A LOT WORSE,' blasted Flora again.

'Yes, sorry!' said Wogan, looking terrified. 'A lot worse! Sorry!'

'That's OK,' said Charlie, smiling for the first time in what felt like forever. 'I haven't learned the spellings either, so we're both in big trouble!'

But even as he spoke, Charlie found that he really didn't care about the spellings very much.

'So,' said Wogan, desperate to change the subject. 'What happened after your parents told you?'

'Well,' said Charlie. 'That's where things started getting really weird . . .'

***

When his parents had finished talking, explaining all the reasons why separating was the right thing to do and why it was best for the family, Charlie decided he should get away EXTREMELY FAST before he changed into an animal right there and then in front of his family.

He jumped up from the table and ran out of the kitchen, his parents' cries of 'Charlie!' 'Don't run off!' and 'Sit down and talk to us!' ringing in his ears. He bounded up the stairs as fast as he could, dived into his room, slammed the door shut and blocked it, his heart racing.

And as the familiar fiery feelings ripped through his body, Charlie realized something extraordinary: he didn't want to stop himself from changing. It was like trying to stop the tide or blowing against the wind. His body wanted to change, and he had to accept it.

And so he did.

His body stretched and shrank, expanded and contracted, and when Charlie caught sight of himself in the mirror, he saw something utterly extraordinary.

He was changing, but not just into an animal.

He was changing into *lots* of animals.

All at the same time.

Bang! The top half of him was a lion, the bottom half was a frog.

Bang! His head was a giant fish, his body a fuzzy koala.

Bang! His top half was a duck-billed platypus, his bottom half was a duck-billed platypus.[12]

[12] Duck-billed platypuses are one of the weirdest creatures on the planet. They have the bill of a duck, the tail of a beaver and the feet of an otter. The first scientists to see a preserved platypus thought it was a fake, made of lots of different animals sewn together! They are also one of the very few mammals that lay eggs. Now, if you are ever tempted to go up to a platypus and say 'Hey, ugly-butt, you're one of the weirdest creatures on the planet and you look like lots of different animals sewn together', I wouldn't – they have a poisonous spur on the foot which can give one of the most painful stings in the world. It's agonizing, the pain can last for months and there's nothing doctors can do about it!

Bang! From the waist up, he was a gigantic grizzly bear, below the waist stuck out a pair of skinny chicken legs.[13]

Again and again he changed, until gradually the changes began to slow down and finally stop.

There, looking back at Charlie from the mirror, was a perfectly normal front end of a cat. Attached to a perfectly normal body of an octopus. Together they were far from normal.

Charlie was half cat, half octopus.[14]

'Well, well, well,' came a voice from behind Charlie. He turned, whiskers twitching, eight legs wriggling.

---

[13] Oooh, chicken-watchers, Charlie nearly changed into a chicken there! But not all the way, so it didn't count.

[14] The obvious joke here would be that Charlie was an octopussy. But *Octopussy* was the title for a terrible James Bond film, so I can't. Thanks a lot, terrible James Bond film.

The voice had come from Chairman Meow, who was sitting on the lid of Charlie's laundry basket wearing the most disdainful and disgusted look his cat-face could muster.[15]

'Congratulations, human,' Chairman Meow continued. 'You have somehow made yourself even more repulsive than you were before. You are so disgusting, you might actually cause me to sick up a fur ball. And that fur ball would still be more pleasant-looking than you.'

---

[15] And considering cats always look disdainful and disgusted, that's saying something.

'How lovely to speak to you too, Chairman Meow.'

'I told you, my name is not Chairman Meow! It is Deathclaw Litterborn of the House Felis, the First of His Name, the –'

'Oh, don't start all that again,' Charlie said, eight legs flapping.

Chairman Meow started licking himself clean, furiously. Charlie suddenly realized he was also very dirty and in need of a thorough wash. He started licking his tentacles urgently.

'I was in the middle of my eighth sleep of the day and you come barging in here smelling like an enormous dog poo left out in the sun,' Chairman Meow continued, licking himself ferociously. 'Here's an idea: have you ever considered going away?'

'Going away?'

'Yes, going far, far away, and never coming

back? You won't be missed. Just like the other cat.'

'What do you mean, "like the other cat"?'

'The cat that sits in boxes. It has been gone for two days.'

'The Great Catsby is missing?' Charlie's tentacles rippled in shock, and he accidentally squirted a jet of ink all over his bedroom floor. 'Oops. Pardon me.'

Chairman Meow sneered. 'Typical! You didn't even realize the other cat had gone! You humans are so wrapped up in your own little worlds.'

'Well . . . will you help me look for him?'

'Absolutely not. I despise that other cat almost as much as I despise you.'

'You're horrible, Chairman Meow.'

'Says the disgusting half-cat half-octopus creature.'

'Fair point.'

'I *could* give you a clue where the cat is, though.'

'Great!'

'But I won't.'

'I hate you, Chairman Meow.'

CHAPTER 5

Flora gave a great gasp of shock.

'So the Great Catsby is missing as well?'

'What do you mean, "as well"?' Wogan asked.

'First the chinchillas went missing from the zoo,' said Flora. 'Then the pets from town. And now the Great Catsby too? There's something going on here, boys, and no mistake.'

'What is it?' asked Wogan.

'I'm not sure yet,' said Flora, staring off into the distance. 'I'm not sure . . .'

'You said that twice. You must *really* not be sure,' said Wogan.

'You know Flora,' said Mohsen. 'She'll get

there in the end. She loves a good mystery. She's like the Sherlock Holmes of our school. Remember the Case of My Missing Easter Egg?'

'Err . . . yes,' replied Wogan.

'How Flora quickly deduced you had eaten it because you had chocolate all over your face and were complaining of a stomachache?'

'Yes, well . . .'

'And what about the Case of the Spiders All Over My Bedroom, when my bedroom was suddenly filled with spiders, and Flora worked it out because she asked you if you'd forgotten to close the lid on your spider collection box, and you started crying and confessed everything? Flora is so clever. She'll definitely work it out.' Mohsen shook his head, smiling. 'I was still finding spiders under my pillow *months* later. What fun times we have together, guys, don't we?'

'So,' said Charlie. 'Do you have any ideas at all, Flor?'

'Hmm,' hmmed Flora. 'Well, there is *one* clue . . .'

'You see!' said Mohsen, thumping his palm. 'I knew she'd solve the case!'

'I haven't solved anything yet!'

'No. But you *nearly* have.'

'I'm nowhere near.'

'What's the clue, Flora?' asked Charlie.

'OK, so remember the signs about the missing pets? Well, one of them said they'd discovered paw prints in the garden. What if a big wild animal is attacking people's pets?'

Mohsen nodded. 'And didn't the sign say *they were feline paw prints*? *Like a lion or a* tiger?'

Charlie shook his head. 'A lion would have had to escape from the zoo, and I'm sure the police would know if that had happened.'

'So it CAN'T be that,' said Wogan. 'Flora, you're a terrible detective.'

'It's true that it can't have escaped from the

zoo,' replied Flora. 'But maybe it's a wild animal the police don't know about.'

'But where would that have come fr–' Mohsen stopped in his tracks, and turned to Charlie, his eyes going wide. 'It's you!'

'What's me?' asked Charlie, looking around.

'You've been turning into a lion and eating all the missing animals!'

Wogan jumped up, pointing at Charlie accusingly. 'Daisy is going to be FURIOUS when she hears you scoffed all the chinchillas!'

'No! That's not what I meant!' cried Flora. 'I wasn't saying it was Charlie! I just meant maybe there's a wild panther or something roaming about. You know, you hear about that sort of thing.'

'It's possible,' said Mohsen. 'But I think my Charlie theory makes much more sense.'

'I have NOT been turning into a lion, and eating cats and chinchillas, thank you very

much!' shouted Charlie. 'I can't believe you think I would do that.'

'OK . . .' said Mohsen, eyes still narrowed with suspicion.

'I can see your eyes still narrowed with suspicion, Mohsen,' said Charlie.

'Fine,' said Mohsen, forcing his eyes open wider.

The gang had reached the school gates. As they entered, Lola ran up to them.

'Hi, guys,' said Lola.

'Hello, Lola,' said Wogan, Flora and Charlie.

'Lello, Hola,' Mohsen stammered in a high voice, then slapped himself on the forehead.

'Really sorry, Wogan,' said Lola. 'But Daisy has asked me to tell you that she doesn't want to go to the dance with you any more.'

'Oh,' said Wogan.

'But, Mohsen,' said Lola.

'Yes,' yelped Mohsen. 'That's me.'

'Would *you* like to go with *me*?'

'I . . . err . . . yes.'

'Great!'

And without another word, Lola skipped off.

Charlie put his arm around Wogan. 'Never mind! I don't have anyone to go to the dance with either!'

Flora swallowed. 'Charlie, would you –'

'Yeah,' interrupted Wogan, glumly. 'Maybe you and I should go to the dance together. No one else will go with us.'

'Not a bad idea, that,' Charlie agreed. 'What were you saying, Flor?'

Flora shook her head. 'Nothing,' she said quietly.

Wogan's day did not get any better, what with the feared spelling test after lunch. He came out, shaking his head and muttering, 'This is the actual worst day of my life.'

Charlie agreed.

It wasn't made any better when Dylan walked out right behind them.

'You'd have to be a right dummy to have messed that test up. It was SO easy,' he gloated, a smug smile plastered across his face.

'What's that plastered across your face?' asked Charlie.

'Erm . . . a smug smile?' replied Dylan.

'No, next to it,' Charlie said, pointing to a big plaster on Dylan's cheek.

'Oh that! I . . . erm . . . fell over and grazed myself,' Dylan replied. 'Anyway, must dash,' he continued. 'Great talking to you. Byeee!'

And Dylan ran off as fast as possible.

'What a weirdo,' said Wogan, shaking his head.

Charlie couldn't disagree. Dylan *was* acting even weirder than usual.

Before they could think any further about it, though, Flora and Mohsen came running up.

'Have you heard?' Flora said, breathlessly.

'What?' said Wogan, full of breath.

'The school chickens have gone missing,' said Flora. 'Disappeared. Vanished. Stolen. Or eaten. There were . . .' Flora lowered her voice to a conspiratorial whisper. 'There were *feathers* all over the coop.'

Mohsen stabbed a finger at Charlie. 'You've been in school today! You could have eaten the chickens!'

'What are you talking about?' asked Charlie. 'It couldn't have been me! I've been with at least one of you guys all day!'

'The chickens were actually attacked yesterday night,' said Flora. 'But it was only noticed this morning. Apparently there's video footage!'

'So what happened then?' asked Charlie. 'Who was it?'

'I don't know. I haven't seen the video. I asked Mr Wind if I could and he said he doesn't want anyone to see it in case it causes panic.'

'What does that mean?' asked Mohsen. 'Why would he say that? *Now* I'm panicking.'

'We have to see that footage,' Flora said, gravely. 'Something big is happening in this town and we need to get to the bottom of it.'

'And how are we supposed to see the footage? Where is it?' asked Charlie, not wanting to know the answer.

'It's on the computers in the security office,' replied Flora.

'And that means . . . ?'

'That means we have to break into the security office, of course,' replied Flora.

'Break into somewhere? Well, what an enormous surprise,' said Charlie, sounding not in the least surprised.

***

It didn't take long for the gang to concoct a plan.[16] The plan was:

1. Charlie changes into an animal.

2. Somehow they break into the office.

It wasn't a very detailed plan, but the four friends were all very happy with it.

They took the opportunity at lunch break.

They waited for the coast to be clear outside the security office, which was fortunately down a quiet corridor.

'OK, Charlie,' said Flora. 'It's time to do

---

[16] Well, it was Flora, of course.

your thing. We need you to break the door down. So think strong.'

Charlie closed his eyes. His darkest thoughts were so near the surface now – *my family is breaking up* – he began to change almost at once. In his mind, Charlie kept a clear picture of the strongest animal he knew – a gorilla – and was relieved when he started to feel hair sprouting all over his body. But the relief was short-lived as he began shrinking instead of growing. And once he had gone from small to *very* small to really, really tiny, he knew he definitely wasn't turning into a gorilla.

From what he could see of himself, he looked like a monkey of some sort but he was so small that couldn't be right, could it? He looked up at his three friends, who were staring at him in astonished silence. Then . . .

'OH MY GOSH HE IS SO ADORABLE!'
squealed Flora.

'HE'S SO TEENY AND FLUFFY!'
squealed Wogan.

'I WANT TO SMUSH HIM ALL UP, HE'S
SO CUTE!' squealed Mohsen.

Guys, thought Charlie. *Can we please stop all the squealing?*

'What IS he? He's beautiful!' Wogan said, with a sappy look on his face.

'He's the cutest, most icklest, sweetest finger monkey!'[17] replied Flora, with an even sappier look on her face.[18]

Ah, come on now, guys, squeaked Charlie. *Pull yourselves together!*

'Can we pick him up?' asked Wogan.

'Yes, let's! Just a quick cuddle!' Flora bent down and scooped Charlie off the ground, then started cuddling him.

---

[17] Flora was right – the animal Charlie had turned into is known as a finger monkey (because it's a monkey that's about the size of a finger) but its real name is the pygmy marmoset. And you should look up pictures of them RIGHT NOW because they are SO SO SWEET AND GORGEOUS AND I WANT ONNNNE!!!

I'm sorry. I lost myself for a moment there. Won't happen again.

[18] Come on, Flora. Pull yourself together. Stop being so silly and sappy. It's only A REAL-LIFE GORGEOUS SWEET TINY MONKEY THAT ACTUALLY IS SO SMALL IT CAN CLING ON TO YOUR FINGER – AAAHHH, SO CUUUUUTE!

Once again, I'm sorry. That really won't happen again.

Stop it, guys! thought Charlie crossly. *We're on an important mission here. Focus!*

'Oh he's so fuzzy!' cried Flora, snuggling Charlie the finger monkey.

'It's my turn!' shouted Wogan, trying to snatch Charlie from Flora.

'Be careful! You'll drop him!' shouted Flora.

'Give him here!' shouted Wogan, managing to tug Charlie away from Flora and cuddling him in the crook of his neck.

'Give him back!' yelled Flora, trying to grab him.

'It's not fair!' Mohsen shouted, stamping his foot. 'It's *my* turn to cuddle Charlie! And that's something I never thought I would say.'

Right, thought Charlie, who was starting to worry he might get pulled apart. *That is it! I've had enough!*

Charlie, who was now very good at changing quickly, turned back to himself so fast he was

Charlie again before Wogan could put him down.

So it was unfortunate that Daisy and Lola chose that exact moment to come round the corner, to find Wogan cradling his best friend in his arms like an overgrown baby. As soon as Wogan saw Daisy staring, he dropped Charlie on the floor.

'Ow!' cried Charlie. 'That hurt!'

'Hi, Daisy!' said Wogan in a strangled voice.

'Er, hi,' replied Daisy. 'What are you guys up to?'

'Um, just trying to break into the office to see if we can find out what happened to the school chickens,' Wogan said, trying to sound brave. 'But the security is impregnable,' he continued, thumping his palm against the door in frustration. 'It's like a bank vault.'

Daisy walked over, turned the handle and the door opened.

'Did you even *try* opening it?' she asked.
'They never lock this door. See you!'

Daisy and Lola walked off, leaving the four friends in a state of shocked silence. And then the silence broke into a sudden pile-up of arguments.

'I thought you checked the door!'

'I thought Flora did it! She's supposed to be the clever one!'

'What? I can't think of EVERYTHING!'

'I didn't even get a chance to cuddle Charlie!'

'You all went bananas and nearly pulled me in two!'

'So what? You really embarrassed me in front of Daisy, so thanks VERY much!'

'You dropped me! On the floor!'

'She saw me cuddling you! What was I supposed to do? KEEP cuddling you? She'd never let me go to the dance with her then!'

The friends kept arguing for a while longer until slowly they all began to see the ridiculousness of the situation and the shouting turned into laughter.[19]

'Shall we go in?' Flora smiled, opening the

---

[19] Most arguments seem ridiculous after enough time has passed. Next time you're having an argument, try and think if it would look ridiculous after, say, a year? Definitely. A month? Almost certainly. A day? Probably. You see, most arguments are ridiculous but they are easy to get caught up in at the time.

door widely and giving a little bow.

They all piled into the small room and shut the door behind them. It was dimly lit, hot, dusty and full of whirring computers. A couple of computer screens showed flickering security footage of various parts of the school, all branded with the logo of Van der Gruyne Industries (who sold most of the security systems in town).

They dived on to one of the computers, and after a few minutes of searching they found the file containing the footage of the camera that covered the school field where the chicken coop sat. They clicked play, hardly daring to breathe.

They watched it on fast forward until Mohsen suddenly shouted, 'Stop!'

'There!' he said. 'At the back of the field!'

Charlie let the video play at normal speed. Mohsen was right, there was movement in the background – a brown shape clambering over the school fence. It seemed to get a leg caught at

the top and then fell to the ground like a sack of rocks. The brown shape lay stunned for a moment, then picked itself up and lumbered forward through the playground. Although the footage was shaky and grainy, the shape looked like . . .

'Is that a *bear*?' asked Flora.

Mohsen nodded. 'I mean, it's small but it looks like a bear.'

'A koala?' suggested Wogan.

'No, it's bigger than a koala,' said Flora. 'Maybe a baby grizzly?'

'What's a baby grizzly bear doing round here?' asked Wogan.

No one had an answer to that, so they watched in silence as the bear lurched towards the chicken coop. They braced themselves to watch the bear eat the chickens, but then, just as it reached the coop, the footage abruptly cut out.

'What happened?' asked Mohsen.

'The recording stops there,' replied Charlie, desperately clicking the mouse. 'Just at the wrong moment.'

'We should get Dylan to tell his dad to mend his rubbish security cameras,' said Wogan.

'Well, at least we know it was a bear that ate the chickens,' said Mohsen.

'Hmm,' hmmed Flora.

'I had a feeling you were going to hmm,' said Mohsen. 'It's been ages since you hmmed, so I thought you were due one.'

Wogan nodded. 'Yeah, Flora. You're getting a bit predictable with the hmming. Maybe you could introduce a few new noises? Like . . . "Ooooooh"?'

'Yes,' agreed Mohsen. 'Or . . . "Ah-hah!"'

'Good one,' Wogan said. 'Or how about –'

'DO YOU WANT TO HEAR WHY I HMMED OR NOT?' Flora snapped, glaring at

Mohsen and Wogan. They nodded, mouths clamped tight shut.

'Well,' continued Flora, 'I was thinking that it certainly looks like some sort of bear got to the chickens. But if you remember, whoever wrote the lost pet notice said it was a large *feline* paw print that they found, like a lion or a tiger. Bear prints are totally different.'

'How on *earth* do you know all this stuff?' asked Mohsen admiringly.

'So what are you saying, Flor?' said Charlie.

'I'm saying it's highly unlikely there's both a bear AND a lion on the loose.'

'Ah, so you *do* think Charlie's eating chickens and pets and cute little zoo animals and stuff?' asked Mohsen.

'WHAT?' Charlie exploded. 'I CAN'T –'

'No!' shouted Flora, looking red in the face. 'I'm sure it isn't Charlie.'

'Even though all the evidence points towards

him,' said Wogan, matter-of-factly.

'IT WASN'T ME!'

'Of COURSE it wasn't, Charlie,' said Flora, soothingly. 'I'm most definitely *not* saying it was you, thank you very much, Wogan and Mohsen. I'm saying there's something else going on. We just need to work out *what*. A bear AND a lion? Unlikely. There has to be some other explanation.'

The door of the office suddenly burst open,

and Mr Wind and Miss Fyre fell in, laughing.

When they saw the four friends, they froze.

'Wha-wha-what are you children doing in here?' Mr Wind stammered.

The friends found they didn't have a single excuse.

'Mr Wind and I were . . . just about to review the security footage,' Miss Fyre said.

The children stared, not daring to say a word.

'WELL!?' shouted Miss Fyre. 'GET OUT OF HERE!'

The children ran out of the office, not looking back.

When they stopped running, Charlie turned to Flora.

'How on earth did we get away with that?'

'I have NO idea,' said Flora.

CHAPTER 6

Charlie was busy in the kitchen on his laptop, glumly designing a 'Missing' poster for the Great Catsby (who *still* hadn't turned up) when his parents dropped their latest, and worst, bombshell. SmoothMove was sitting next to him, playing Zelda on his Nintendo Switch, when their mum and dad walked in, solemn looks on their faces.

'Guys,' said Dad. 'I've something to talk to you about.'

What now? thought Charlie. From his dad's tone of voice, it sounded like more bad news and Charlie didn't think he could face more bad news.

'So,' continued his dad. 'I've been looking for somewhere to live once I move out and I've found a nice flat. It's happened a bit quicker than I'd have liked but I didn't want to lose it, so I've put the deposit down.'

SmoothMove said 'Great' sarcastically under his breath and turned back to his Nintendo. Charlie sat in stunned silence. He had a million things to say but knew if he started speaking, the words would break up in his throat.

'It's a new build,' his dad continued. 'On the estate on the other side of town.'

That's miles away! thought Charlie. *I'll be miles from my friends when I'm staying with him.*

'It's right by a lovely park.'

'When are you moving out?' SmoothMove asked.

'April 21st,' their dad replied. 'You'll both be spending every Wednesday night and weekends with me. And you'll get to share a

bedroom. Which will be fun,' he finished, unconvincingly.

Again, Charlie wanted to say so much: *That's the day after the school dance! How am I supposed to enjoy that now?* And, *If I'm at Dad's every weekend, how can I play with my friends?* And, *Have you even thought about me?* And, *WHY IS THIS HAPPENING? WHY?*

Charlie couldn't bring himself to ask any of those questions, though. He could only turn back to the laptop, hiding his face from his family, blinking back tears.

His mum came up behind him and placed a soft kiss on the top of his head. Try as he might, Charlie couldn't stop the tears beginning to roll down his cheeks. He wiped his eyes, hoping no one had noticed.

Charlie knew he wasn't in danger of changing: he wasn't feeling stressed or afraid or anxious or even angry. Right now, he was just feeling hopelessly sad.

★★★

Please stop being kind to me, Charlie thought. *If you don't stop, I'm going to cry again and I don't want to do that in front of Dylan.*

Charlie was in the playground, his friends

huddling round him.

'There's nothing wrong with crying,' said Flora, seeming to read his mind.

'I know,' said Charlie. 'It's just –'

Mohsen nodded. 'Flora's right. I cry all the time. Like when my grandma died.'

'And like when my older brother went to university. I cried loads,' said Flora.

'Yeah!' said Wogan. 'And like when I went to the toilet last week and caught my winky in my zip. I cried for *ages* then.'

'Wogan!' gasped Flora. 'What is wrong with you?'

'Yes, what's wrong with you, Wogan?' said Mohsen. '"Winky"? That's a very babyish name for it. It's called your "dangly-wangly".'

'No, it isn't! It's called a "winky"!' shouted Wogan. 'Although my cousin calls it a "ding-dong",' he continued thoughtfully. 'So I –'

'Can you STOP talking about winkies and

dangly-wanglies and ding-dongs?' blurted Flora. 'What is *wrong* with you? We are trying to make Charlie feel better, if you hadn't forgotten!'

'What are you four imbeciles talking about then?' Dylan had sidled up without anyone noticing. He still had a plaster on his face.

'Nothing!' they all replied instantly.

'Yeah, that doesn't sound suspicious at all. Anyway,' said Dylan, 'Charlie, I want a word with you. Alone.'

Charlie shrugged at his friends and walked into the corridor with Dylan, who Charlie noticed was limping.

'Why are you limping?'

'I . . . erm . . . don't know.'

'What do you mean, you don't know?'

'I mean, of course I know! I have a sore leg because . . . I fell off a . . . unicycle.'

'You fell off a *unicycle*?'

'Look, it doesn't matter. That's not why I wanted to talk to you.'

'Yeah, what do you want, Van der Gruyne?' Charlie eyed Dylan suspiciously.

'I just heard your parents were separating.'

'And?'

'Well, I know what it's like.'

'How?' Charlie snapped. 'Your parents are still together.'

'I know. But sometimes I don't think they should be.'

A long look passed between them, deep and unspoken.

'Oi, Charlie!' Wogan shouted suddenly, breaking the silence, his head poking out of the classroom door. 'When you've finished talking to that useless sack of soggy broccoli, can you help me with the spellings?'

Dylan was back to sneering at Charlie, as if he had just remembered he hated him.

'But don't think this changes anything between us, McGuffin,' Dylan snarled, extra venom in his voice. 'We're still mortal enemies.'

'But *why*?'

'Because,' said Dylan. 'I'm evil. On the outside, anyway. But I'm like an onion, McGuffin. I have layers. And peel those layers back and . . . I'm exactly the same evil onion in the middle, and I also make you cry.'

'But you don't *have* to be an evil onion!'

'Of course I do,' said Dylan, a hint of weariness and resignation in his voice. 'Because every story needs a hero and a villain. And I am this story's villain.'

'Dylan. You're not a villain. You're a schoolboy who watches too many movies.'

'Oh, Charlie. You have NO idea how much of a villain I am. You don't even know *what* you don't know. That's how much you don't know.'

'Oh, I know EXACTLY how much I don't know.'

But little did Charlie know how little he knew about how little he knew.

Dylan limped off, cackling like a wicked witch who had changed herself into a wicked limping schoolboy.

Charlie followed a moment later, once again despairing at Dylan. But he couldn't help feeling a little disturbed by what Dylan had said. He was left with a small, nagging suspicion that he actually *didn't* know how much he didn't know about how much he didn't know.

He arrived back in his classroom and his three friends were looking at him, clearly burning with curiosity.

'What was *that* about?' Flora asked.

'Nothing,' replied Charlie sullenly.

'What do you mean, "nothing"? It had to have been about *something*.'

But before Charlie could say anything more, Daisy walked up to them.

'Hello, you lot,' she said. 'Been struggling to open any other doors recently?'

'HA HA HA HA!' Wogan laughed, rather too loudly.

'So,' continued Daisy, ignoring Wogan. 'Message for Mohsen: Mohsen, Lola says she's really sorry but she can't go to the school dance with you.'

'Ah,' said Mohsen, visibly deflating, like an old balloon. 'OK,' he added to Daisy's back as she walked off.

Wogan put his arm round Mohsen. 'I feel your pain.'

'You know,' said Flora. 'Those girls are really starting to annoy me.'

★★★

The following Sunday, Mohsen, Wogan and Charlie were piling into the back of the McGuffin family car. Charlie's mum was dropping Mohsen and Wogan back home after a play date and the boys were discussing the school dance.

'There is absolutely no way I'm doing *any* dancing,' announced Mohsen. 'I've got two left feet.'

'What?' gasped Wogan, looking down. 'I've never noticed! How do you get shoes that fit?'

'I don't *actually* have two left feet. It's just a phrase. It means –'

'Shush!' blurted out Charlie, suddenly. 'Mum, turn up the radio!'

'What –' Mohsen started.

'Just listen!' Charlie said.

Charlie's mum turned up the radio.

'And we're going over now live to the zoo, following earlier reports of a break-in there,' said the news presenter in a grave voice. 'Holly, what can you tell us?'

'Well, Dan,' Holly the reporter replied. 'It does indeed appear that the zoo was broken into yesterday night and a number of animals have disappeared.'

'And could you tell us what animals have been stolen?' Dan asked.

'Yes, I could, Dan.'

'Well . . . *will* you tell us what animals have been stolen?'

'Ah yes,' replied Holly. 'I see. Of course. A number of penguins are missing, together with two eagles, a goat and a llama. Some gnawed bones were found in the Pit of Penguins, leading police to fear the worst. The zookeepers are distraught and can't imagine who – or *what* – is behind it.'

'Did you say "what", Holly?' Dan asked, his voice laced with shock.

'That's right, Dan. One theory the police are working on is that a wild animal broke into the zoo and ate these poor creatures. Or worse.'

'Worse?' asked Dan. 'What could be worse than being eaten by a wild animal?'

'Being eaten by two wild animals, Dan,' replied Holly. 'And police are looking for evidence that there could be more than one animal terrorizing our town. Unfortunately, the zoo's security system seems to have broken, so there is no video footage that the police can look at to confirm this theory.'

'What extraordinary bad luck,' said Dan. 'Could there be any connection between this latest attack and the polar bear that was sighted in a residential area a few months ago?'

Holly nodded. 'We can't rule it out. The ravenous beast – or beasts – could be any sort of wild animal – a polar bear, a tiger, even a large dog. Rest assured, though, the police are following every possible lead.'

'I don't think this is a time for jokes, Holly.'

'I'm sorry, Dan.'

'Well, Holly, let's hope the animals are soon found safe and well, and we can put this beastly business behind us.'

'I thought you said this wasn't a time for jokes, Dan.'

'You're right, Holly. I'd like to apologize to all listeners.'

Charlie gasped. 'OK, Mum, you can turn it down now.' He turned to his friends and whispered anxiously. 'OK, I'm REALLY worried about the Great Catsby now!'

Mohsen and Wogan looked back at Charlie with very serious faces.

'What are you both looking at?'

'Charlie,' said Wogan slowly. 'More animals possibly eaten? In unexplained circumstances? And we were all just at the zoo the other day.'

'And? So what?' Charlie replied crossly.

'Maybe,' said Mohsen gently. 'Maybe it's

you but you don't remember doing it.'

'It wouldn't be your fault then,' Wogan added quickly. 'You wouldn't be to blame.'

'IT'S NOT ME!' Charlie shouted.

'What's not you, dear?' asked Charlie's mum.

'Nothing, Mum,' Charlie replied, then turned back to his friends and hissed, 'OK, I know it looks suspicious, but I PROMISE it's not me.'

'Well, anyway,' said Mohsen. 'I bet I know what Flora's going to want to do.'

'You're right,' groaned Charlie. 'I can already guess what her plan's going to be . . .'

'What?' asked Wogan.

★★★

'So, here's the plan,' announced Flora at school the next day. 'We break into the zoo!'

'What an enormous surprise,' said Charlie, once again sounding the very opposite of surprised.

'That's right, Charlie. What a tremendous shock,' agreed Mohsen.

Wogan clapped his hands. 'You guys were right!'

'What are you talking about?' asked Flora, looking perplexed.

'We've noticed that EVERY time we need a plan, you ALWAYS say that we have to break into somewhere,' said Wogan.

'Well if anybody has any better suggestions, I am quite open to hearing them,' said Flora, crossing her arms.

'No!' cried Charlie. 'It's a great plan, Flora!'

Dylan suddenly walked past, glaring at them, dragging a sack behind him. He had a bandage wrapped round his head, and scratches all over his face.

'What happened to *him*?' Charlie said.

'Fell off a skateboard, apparently,' replied Mohsen.

'Since when does Dylan skateboard?' asked Charlie. 'He said he fell off a unicycle the other day as well. And why's he by himself all the time these days?'

'Reckon he must have had a falling-out with Teddy. I haven't seen them together in ages,'

Mohsen replied. 'In fact, I haven't seen him playing with *anybody* in ages.'

The gang were quiet for a moment.

'Poor Dylan,' said Flora.

'What do you mean, "Poor Dylan"?' gasped Wogan. 'Have you forgotten what a total and complete doofus-head he is?!'

'I'm not saying he *isn't* a total and complete doofus-head,' said Flora. 'But it can't be nice being alone all the time.'

That sent the gang quiet again, lost in thought for a moment, until Charlie broke the silence.

'Anyway, back to the plan,' he said. 'Why do we need to break into the zoo?' he asked. 'We already know the security system didn't get any video footage.'

'Ah!' said Flora, waggling her eyebrows. 'We have a secret weapon . . .'

'Is it a rocket launcher?' asked Wogan. 'I bet it's a rocket launcher.'

'No, Wogan. It isn't,' replied Flora to Wogan, who looked crestfallen. 'It's Charlie.'

'Argh, he's *rubbish* compared to a rocket launcher.'

Flora ignored him.

'So, here's what we do: we break in and Charlie changes into an animal, then asks the other animals if they saw anything. Or *anyone*.'

'Now, *that*,' said Charlie, 'is actually quite a brilliant plan.'

A small smile sneaked on to Flora's face.

'Totally!' said Mohsen. 'We can finally find out if it's Charlie eating the animals!'

'IT'S NOT ME!'

Puffin Books

80 Strand

London

Dear Mr Copeland,

Just to remind you, we are half-way through this book, and still no mammoths.

We don't believe that you will pull the same stunt again – not after how much trouble you caused last time.

So, we very much look forward to seeing Charlie turn into a mammoth very soon!

Yours sincerely,

The Publisher

Dear Puffin Books,

Yup – don't you worry. Charlie will be turning into a mammoth really, really soon. Promise.

Yours truthfully, your honest author,

Sam Copeland

CHAPTER 7

O ver the next few days, several more animals – this time dogs – went missing from addresses all across town, and finally the newspapers were joining the dots.

'Pilfering Pet-Predator Poaches Pooches!' read one headline.

'Dog-Gone Mystery Sends Town Barking Mad!' read another.

'Interest Rates Set to Rise as Inflation Slows Down!' read another, which only ever printed the really boring news.

The police were baffled. All sorts of animals were going missing and there was a growing collection of conflicting clues: bones in the Pit of Penguins at the zoo, the video of a small bear at the school and large feline footprints in people's back gardens – it seemed like the whole town had gone wild.

Charlie's friends had stopped accusing him directly, but he could see – even behind Flora's eyes and despite her strenuous denials – that there was still doubt there.

It was agreed that they should break into the zoo as soon as possible.

'So we can finally found out the truth about Charlie,' said Mohsen.

'No!' said Flora, glancing at Charlie. 'So we can stop more animals from getting eaten!'

So the following day, the four friends found themselves outside the zoo just after closing time. Their faces were stern, ready for action.

'Right,' said Flora. 'We need to be extra careful to make sure nobody sees Charlie changing now. Because if anybody else finds out, they're going to think he's the one eating the animals.'

'Ah,' said Wogan. 'There might be a little problem with –'

'It's fine, Flora,' Mohsen was simultaneously replying. 'Apart from us, only Dylan knows about Charlie's powers. And no one is going to believe him. So as long as we keep completely quiet, everything will be OK.'

'Yes, about that,' said Wogan. 'There's a chance I might have –'

'You're right, Mohsen,' said Flora. 'I shouldn't worry. It's not like any of us would be stupid enough to blab to anyone.'

'Hi, guys!' said a voice suddenly.

Three of the four friends swung round in shock; the fourth looked guilty. It was Daisy and Lola.

'Erm, hi. What are you doing here?' asked Flora.

'We're here to help break into the zoo,' said Daisy brightly.

'To see if it's Charlie eating all the animals,' explained Lola. 'You know, when he changes into an animal himself.'

'H-h-how did you . . . ?' stammered Flora.

'Thanks for inviting us, Wogan!' said Daisy. 'Hey, why are you running away?'

'WOGAN! COME BACK HERE IMMEDIATELY!' roared Flora.

Wogan slunk back to the gang, a look of terror on his face.

'I-I-I . . .' Wogan stuttered.

'DO NOT SAY A WORD,' Flora roared again.

'Look,' said Charlie, glaring at Wogan. 'It can't be helped now, so let's carry on and find out what's happening, OK? Anybody have an idea how to get in?'

Charlie looked up at the huge wire fence that confronted them.

'Well, we could just use the key,' said Lola, holding up a key.

'What's that?' asked Charlie.

'It's the key,' replied Lola, looking at Charlie as if he was simple. 'To the zoo.'

'H-h-how . . . ?' stammered Charlie.

'Do you guys *always* stammer this much?' asked Daisy.

'My mum's one of the hippo-keepers,' said Lola. 'So I borrowed the key when she wasn't looking. I thought it would be useful. You know, since we're breaking into the zoo.'

The four friends stood there in stunned silence until Wogan broke it.

'Yes! That's . . . *That's* why I invited them! I knew Lola's mum worked here so I knew she'd bring the key!'

Five deeply suspicious faces hard-stared at Wogan.

'Anyway!' said Wogan brightly. 'Enough friendly chit-chat. Let's get going!'

Lola sprang into action, unlocked the gate and, a moment later, they were all inside.

'Right,' said Mohsen. 'Which way? Which animals should we talk to first?'

'Well, which were the first to go missing?' asked Charlie.

'Chinchillas,' said Flora. 'Then eagles, a

llama, and some penguins. The penguins would be a good place to start because that's where the bones were found and –'

'Ooooooh! Penguins!' cried Daisy. 'They're so sweet! Let's go to the penguins!'

'Ooooooh!' agreed Wogan. 'Yes! Penguins! I love penguins!'

'You've changed your tune,' said Mohsen. 'Last time we were here you said you hated them. You called them greasy-looking –'

Wogan shushed Mohsen, glaring at him.

'Aw!' said Daisy, who fortunately hadn't heard Mohsen. 'You like penguins too, Wogan?'

'Oh yeah,' replied Wogan, nodding. 'Big fan of penguins. Long-time favourite. Definitely.'

'Me too!' beamed Daisy. 'Would you like to come to the school dance, Wogan?'

'I – uh – I guess so! Yes!' Wogan blushed.

Daisy rushed off, smiling.

'You don't mind, do you, Charlie?' asked

Wogan. 'If I go with Daisy?'

'Not at all,' Charlie said.

Flora looked like she was about to lose her temper AGAIN, so before she could say anything, Charlie blurted out, 'OK then! Penguins it is!'

They set off quickly. The zoo was eerily silent, apart from the odd snuffle and squeak from a curious animal. If Charlie wasn't mistaken, there was an air of fear hanging over the place. The animals seemed to be cowering in the corners of their cages as they walked past.

Presently they arrived at the Pit of Penguins, which had about thirty or so penguins huddling round a large pool.

'I'm going to go around the corner to change,' Charlie announced, suddenly feeling shy in front of Daisy and Lola. 'If I'm anything close to a penguin, stick me in there.'

Charlie went behind a small hut, closed his eyes. He remembered how the day after the school dance, his family was going to be torn apart. Nothing would be the same again.

It was easy to change. As the electricity ripped through him, he tried to imagine not just a picture of a penguin, but what it was like to BE a penguin. He imagined the little wings and the curved beak. He imagined standing in the freezing Antarctic wind, warming an egg under his bum.

He was getting smaller – a good sign!

He was growing feathers – another good sign!

He was growing wings!

Was it finally happening? Had he finally worked out how to change into whichever animal he wanted? Charlie thought it was possible, but as he walked out from behind the hut, somehow he didn't quite feel exactly *penguin-y*.

'Oh, Charlie!' grinned Flora as he appeared. 'You've changed into a chicken!'[20]

Charlie clucked in amusement. *That's close enough. A chicken will have to do! I'm getting better!*

'Is that REALLY Charlie?' gasped Daisy.

'Yup,' Wogan nodded proudly.

'Right,' said Flora. 'Let's put him in, so he can talk to the penguins and find out who's been taking these animals.'

'Will they understand him?' Mohsen asked. 'Do penguins speak Chicken?'

'We'd better hope there's some mysterious and never-explained reason why they do,' Wogan answered.

'Wait!' Daisy suddenly shouted. 'With everything that's going on, the penguins might not trust a strange animal! They might think

---

[20] Yes! All those doubters said it would never happen! FINALLY. I mean it's taken nearly three whole books but he did it, chicken-fans. He did it. CHARLIE CHANGED INTO A CHICKEN!

it's come to eat them!'

'What? A carnivorous killer chicken?!' Mohsen asked, looking at Daisy like he so often did at Wogan. 'You think the penguins are going to be scared of *that*?'

Mohsen pointed at Charlie. Charlie clucked, offended.

'Wait, maybe Daisy has a point . . .' Flora said, rubbing her chin. 'We could try to make him look a *bit* more penguin-y. Let's see what we can find!'

After a quick search of the area, Lola had found a black bin liner, which they tore up then wrapped round Charlie's body and wings, so they looked black. Flora had found a white paper plate, which they shoved down his front to give him a white chest. And Daisy had found a yellow plastic cup, which, after a bit of shaping, they stuck on the end of Charlie's beak to make it look a bit more like a penguin's.

'You know what?' said Flora standing back and admiring their handiwork. 'He doesn't look half bad!'

'He really does look sort of penguin-y,' agreed Daisy.

'Maybe if you're a REALLY stupid penguin,' Mohsen said.

'Yeah,' agreed Wogan. 'I reckon he looks more like a chicken that fell in a dustbin.'

The girls glared at Wogan and Mohsen.

'But I'm sure the penguins will absolutely go for it!' Wogan added nervously.

'Well, there's only one way to find out!'

Mohsen bent down and plucked Charlie off the floor. Holding him at arm's length, he walked over to the edge of the Pit of Penguins and dropped him inside.

Charlie flapped his wings without any real effect and crash-landed on to the dusty ground. Thirty penguin heads swivelled round, startled.

Then they waddled over to encircle the intruder.

'Vell, vell, vell, Children of the Night,' said one of the penguins. 'Vhat is this that has fallen into our lair?'

'Hi,' said Charlie, not wanting to waste any time. 'I'm –'

'Ssh,' said another penguin, pressing his flipper to Charlie's plastic beak. 'Don't talk. It vill be over soon. Your death vill be quick. Once ve finish drinking your blood.'

'Finish WHAT?!' gasped Charlie.

'What are you talking about? You don't drink blood! You're penguins!'

'Ve are not "pingvins"!' said the tallest penguin, making air-quotation marks with his flippers. 'Ve are vampires!'

'What?! You're not vampires! You're penguins! You're cute, with flappy flippers!'

'Ve are *not* cute!' gasped the penguins indignantly.

'Yes, you are! Look at you! I want to smoosh your cute penguin faces!' Charlie said.

'You try smoosh our face,' said the tall penguin, stepping closer and speaking in a hushed, menacing tone. 'Then ve bite your neck and drink your blood![21] See if

---

[21] You might have realized by now that penguins, although undeniably cute-looking, are in fact cruel, vicious creatures. They are widely regarded as the second-worst animals in the whole world. And who are the worst? Puffins. Puffins are also cute-looking, but are angry, untrustworthy and smell like rotten fish. So if you ever have the misfortune to come into contact with a penguin or a puffin, run the other way. They are the worst of the worst.

you think ve "cute pingvins" then! Ha!'

'You can't bite my neck!' replied Charlie. 'You don't even have any teeth!'

This caused the penguins to mutter angrily among themselves. After a few moments, they turned back to Charlie.

'OK,' said the tallest penguin, holding up a flipper. 'You have point there. But maybe ve are *vampire pingvins* then.'

Charlie stared at the penguins, his beak wide in disbelief.

'Look,' said the penguin, turning round to show off his back. 'Ve have capes. See. Vampire pingvins.'

'That's just your colouring! You have black backs and flippers!'

'It does not matter,' said the tall penguin. 'Ve drink your blood now, chicken!'

The penguins muttered in agreement and took a waddling step towards Charlie.

'What do you mean, "chicken"?' cried Charlie, trying to back away. 'I'm a penguin!'

'Don't be ridiculous. You have chicken accent. You also have ridiculous plastic beak,' the tall penguin said, knocking off Charlie's beak with one swipe of a flipper. 'That disguise vouldn't fool baby vampire pingvin.' The penguins began crowding Charlie even more.

'Aww, how sweet!' Charlie heard Flora say. 'The penguins are trying to cuddle Charlie!'

'OK! I'm sorry! You're right! I'm not a penguin!' Charlie squawked in a completely obvious chicken-voice.

The penguins had now totally surrounded Charlie and started bumping him, hissing, and even attempting little pecks at his neck.

'Oh!' cried Flora. 'Now they're trying to kiss him! So adorable!'

'But I came to find out about the animal that ate the penguins!' Charlie yelled over the hissing.

'You know nothing, chicken!' the tall penguin declared. 'It vas no animal. It vas human child. And it did not eat our brothers. It bundle them into sack, scatter some bones on ground, then go.'

Charlie gasped. 'Was it a boy or a girl?'

'It vas human boy!'

Charlie let this news sink in for a moment. It was a boy who was behind the mysterious disappearances. And they hadn't been eating the animals but kidnapping them and making it *look* like they'd been eaten!

'OK, thanks, guys!' he said. 'You've been loads of help! In the end.'

'Shall ve suck his blood now?' said one of the penguins.

'No!' snapped the tall penguin. 'Ve don't eat chicken! Ve are wegetarian.'

'Are ve? Since vhen?'

'Yes! Remember – ve only eat fish! And

humans. And other pingvins. Apart from that, completely, vun hundred per cent wegetarian!'

Charlie quickly waddled away. As he waddled, he closed his eyes, and breathed in happiness, and thought about his friends waiting for him, and by the time he reached the edge of the Pit of Penguins, he was back to Charlie the boy.

'I think we've got just the break we need,' Charlie grinned, as his friends helped him clamber out of the pit.

CHAPTER 8

The following morning at first break, Flora called a meeting to discuss what they had discovered at the zoo.

'OK, so now we know a boy is involved,' she said, as they guzzled their fruit snacks. 'But does anybody have any ideas who has stolen these animals and *why*?'

'Rustled,' corrected Mohsen.

'Who's Russell?' asked Wogan. 'Is he the one we're looking for? He sounds like a right desperate criminal.'

'Not Russell. *Rustled*,' Mohsen replied. 'Rustling is the proper word for stealing animals.'

'I wonder why,' said Wogan, thoughtfully. 'Maybe they rustle if you hide them under a blanket when you steal them?'

'That's not a bad –'

'Anyway,' interrupted Flora, 'as I was saying, does anybody have any idea why these animals are being *stolen*?'

'Or eaten,' said Wogan.

'Pardon?'

'Just because they're being stolen first doesn't mean they aren't being eaten afterwards.'

'By a *boy*?' asked Flora, despairingly. 'A llama-eating boy? You think there's a chinchilla-munching child stalking our town?'

Wogan looked embarrassed. 'Maybe not.'

'It's much more likely somebody is stealing these animals and trying to make it look like they're being eaten!'

'So here's what we *do* know, then,' said Mohsen. 'A number of animals have gone missing from the zoo and the school and people's gardens. We know that it was a boy that took the animals from the zoo, and a bear that took the chickens from the school. So we are possibly looking for a boy who owns a bear.'

'Or,' said Wogan, waggling a finger in the air, 'a boy who can *change* into a bear? A boy who we *know* changes into animals but who maybe can't remember doing it?'

Mohsen gasped. 'You're saying the wild side has taken over Charlie? That the monster inside him can't be controlled?'

Wogan nodded his head once firmly. 'Exactly.'

'RIGHT, THAT'S IT!' Charlie roared. 'I'VE HAD ENOUGH! I AM NOT A MONSTER! IN CASE YOU HAVE FORGOTTEN, THE GREAT CATSBY IS STILL MISSING! DO YOU THINK I HAVE EATEN MY OWN CAT?'

Charlie was burning with anger. Anger that his friends didn't believe him, anger that his family was falling apart.

'I'm SICK and TIRED of not being trusted! WHY would I be stealing these animals?' Charlie ranted. 'What possible reason could I have for stealing – now let me get this right –' he counted them off on his fingers – 'chinchillas, cats, dogs, chickens, penguins, eagles and a llama? And where on earth do you think I'm keeping them all? I –'

'Shush!' Flora jumped up.

'What do you mean, "shush"? You can't shush me when I'm ranting!'

'Charlie, do shush just for a minute! I'm trying to think!' Flora said, closing her eyes.

Charlie, Wogan and Mohsen fell silent, waiting eagerly to hear what was on Flora's mind. After about eight seconds the silence was too much for Wogan.

'I think she's coming up with an idea,' he whispered.

'That's definitely her ideas face,' replied Mohsen.

'Yeah – it's all scrunched up and red.'

'Yes, she always does that scrunched-up, bright red face like she's straining to do a poo when she's concentrating really hard and –'

'WOULD YOU TWO BLATHERING

CHATTERBOXES BE QUIET FOR JUST ONE MINUTE!' Flora thundered. 'I AM TRYING TO ENTER MY MIND PALACE!'

Mohsen and Wogan froze in terror, not daring to ask what a mind palace was. After a few more moments of intense thinking,[22] Flora opened her eyes and announced calmly:

'I think I know what's going on.'

'What?' asked Wogan and Mohsen urgently.

[22] During which Charlie couldn't help but agree – silently, of course – that Flora did indeed look like she was straining to do a poo.

'You're being framed, Charlie,' Flora said simply.

The three friends gasped in unison. They had a hundred questions but Flora continued to speak.

'Big cat footprints in people's back gardens – that doesn't make sense. Bears in the school playground? That makes even *less* sense. Unless somebody is trying to make it look like there are lots of different animals on the loose in town, eating people's pets. Somebody who knows Charlie can change into animals and is trying to make it look like it's him.'

'But who?' Wogan asked.

'Dylan,' said Charlie. 'Apart from us, he's the only one who knows I can change into animals.'

'Lola and Daisy both know,' said Mohsen.

'They don't count,' replied Flora. 'They only found out *after* the disappearances started.'

'Ah,' said Wogan. 'That's not *exactly* true.

There's a small chance I might have actually told Daisy everything just after the first time you changed.'

The others stared at Wogan.

'In fact, it's more than a small chance. I'm pretty sure I told her. Definitely, I mean. I absolutely did tell her.'

'Great! Now we have two suspects!' groaned Mohsen.

'It's not Daisy!' Wogan blurted out. 'Daisy is sweet and lovely and like an angel!'

'Aww thank you, Wogan! That's sweet of you to say so!'

The friends all swung round to see Daisy and Lola standing right behind them.

'How long have you two been there?' asked Wogan, face glowing bright red.

'Oh, ages,' said Daisy.

'And how do you keep managing to creep up on us like that?' asked Flora.

'So, Lola was wondering,' Daisy continued, ignoring Flora's question, 'whether Mohsen would like to come to the dance with her.'

Flora slapped her forehead. 'Oh, for goodness' –'

Mohsen stared down at one of his two left feet and muttered 'yes'.

'Honestly,' continued Flora. 'I'm starting to think I might not even bother going to this ridiculous dance!'

The thought of Flora not being at the dance gave Charlie a sudden hollow feeling in his chest.

'Anyway,' Charlie said quietly, getting back to the matter in hand. 'It has to be Dylan. He hates me *and* he's been acting really weird lately.'

'Weird how?' asked Mohsen.

'Well, he's always sneaking around by himself for a start. And every time I see him, he seems to have some new injury.'

'You reckon he's been getting hurt stealing the animals?' asked Mohsen.

'Exactly!' replied Charlie. 'And I keep seeing him carrying sacks and looking really guilty!'

'OK!' said Flora. 'We have a number one suspect!'

Mohsen suddenly let out a huge gasp and slapped his forehead.

'The security cameras!'

'What about the security cameras?' asked Flora.

'Who makes them all, Flora?'

'Of course!' Flora jumped up. 'Van der Gruyne Industries! Dylan's dad's company! Dylan must have some way of controlling the cameras, so no one can see it's really him kidnapping the animals! Why didn't I think of that! Oh, Mohsen, you are clever!'

Mohsen blushed. 'It was actually Wogan who gave me the idea. Back when we were watching the video of the bear. He said we should complain to Dylan's dad about the security camera breaking. And then I remembered the cameras weren't working at the zoo either.'

'I knew it!' said Wogan to Daisy. 'I always thought I was the clever one in the gang and this just proves it!'

Daisy beamed. 'Well done! Wogan, you're a genius!'

'People always call me that!'

'People always call you a genius?' asked Flora, incredulously.

'No. People always call me Wogan.'

'Anyway!' Flora clapped her hands. 'We have to find out exactly what Dylan is planning and why.'

'Can we help?' asked Daisy.

Flora thought for a moment. 'Well, you two are very good at sneaking up on people,' she said. 'So you'll make great spies!' she added with a wide smile.

***

The six friends split into pairs to take it in turns to secretly watch Dylan. At Wogan's suggestion, he paired off with Daisy, Mohsen paired with Lola and Charlie paired with Flora.

Flora and Charlie went first. For the rest of break, they sneaked around behind Dylan, following his every move. He seemed nervous, constantly looking behind him, but Charlie and Flora managed to stay hidden. Finally, Dylan reached the boys' changing room, looked round once again and sneaked in. Charlie and Flora cracked the changing-room door open a tiny bit and peeked in. Dylan was at a locker and started rummaging inside, looking extremely suspicious.

'We need to see what's in there, Charlie!' Flora whispered.

Charlie nodded in agreement.

Dylan slammed the locker shut before they could see anything and rushed out of the changing room, nearly knocking over Charlie and Flora in the process.

'What do you two nincompoops think you're doing, creeping round the boys' changing room?' Dylan sneered.

'We know you're up to something, Van der Gruyne! And we're going to stop you!' Charlie said, determination in his voice.

'Stop me? It's far too late for that! Your fate, McGuffin, has already been sealed.'

'The only thing that's going to be sealed is your mouth when we stop your plan!' said Flora.

'Oh! Charlie's little girlfriend is sooo brave! I'm shaking in my boots!'

'She is NOT my girlfriend!' Charlie shot back.

'Yeah, right.' Dylan grinned meanly. 'I hope you two lovebirds enjoy the school dance – it's going to be wild!'

And with that, he stalked off, sniggering.

Charlie looked at Flora, ready to talk about what had just happened, but despite her smiling brightly at him, he saw there was a different emotion hidden deep in Flora's eyes. If he wasn't mistaken, it was sadness.

And that caused a little shadow to pass over Charlie.

★★★

'Right, guys! What do we know?' said Mohsen, when they all met up at the end of the day. 'Because Lola and I have discovered some *crazy* information!'

'Great!' said Flora. 'Why don't you go first and then we can tell you what we found out!'

'Right, so me and Lola were following Dylan during lunch and you'll never guess where he went.'

'Erm . . . the roof of the school!' guessed Wogan. 'No! The . . . staff room! No . . . the swimming pool!'

'Our school doesn't have a swimming pool, Wogan,' sighed Flora.

'The goat pen then!'

'We don't have a goat pen, either.'

'The . . . astronomy tower?'

'Or one of those.'

'Gah! Our school is rubbish! I don't know! Where *has* Dylan been going then?'

'Well,' said Mohsen. 'It was difficult to follow him because he was dead suspicious, but Lola and I were like proper spies, and we tracked him to that door at the end of the computing corridor.'

'I know it,' frowned Charlie. 'The one that's got a great big rusty lock on it.'

'Yeah but Dylan has the key. We watched him unlock it and go in. And we followed him at second break, and he went there again. This time, he was carrying a big sack. We tried following him in but he had locked it from the inside.'

'What IS that place?' asked Flora. 'I've always wondered.'

'So had we,' replied Mohsen. 'So we asked Mr O'Dear.[23] First he screamed at us to get lost and stop being so nosy, then he started ranting about how he'd lost the key, and *then*, just as we were walking away, he shouted after us "And you pesky kids better stay away from that basement!"'

[23] Mr O'Dear, the school caretaker, won Britain's Angriest Man of the Year competition for four years running (1998–2001) until he was disqualified in 2002 for getting so angry he headbutted a judge. Getting disqualified made him even more angry, so he decided to become a school caretaker, as this was the only job where he could be absolutely furious at all times and nobody would question it. Mostly because they were too scared.

'Oh!' cried Flora. 'So that's what Dylan's up to!'

'Of course!' shouted Mohsen, jumping up.

'Yes!' shouted Wogan, jumping up too. 'Hang on – what's he up to?'

'He must be hiding the stolen animals down there!' said Charlie.

'In the school basement?' asked Mohsen. 'Why?'

'Well he needs to keep them *somewhere*. And he can't keep them at home, can he?'

They fell silent for a moment.

'Maybe he's keeping the animals as friends,' said Mohsen finally. 'I haven't seen him speak to a single person in ages. Anyway, what did you guys find out?'

'Not a huge amount,' admitted Charlie. 'But he's definitely hiding something in his locker.'

'Iiinteresting,' replied Mohsen, 'The plot thickens!'

'So,' said Flora, 'we reckon Dylan is up to something suspicious with his locker AND he's keeping stolen animals in the basement. Wogan, what did you and Daisy find out?'

Wogan looked around guiltily. 'I don't think we have time to talk about it, actually,' he said, looking at his watch. 'I think the bell just went. Did anybody else hear the bell? I'm sure I heard the bell. We should go.'

'What are you talking about?' said Flora. 'The bell didn't go! It's nowhere near time! Come on – what did you discover?'

'Yes. Well. We didn't see much of Dylan actually. He was somewhat elusive.'

'What *are* you talking about?' said Flora. 'Wogan – did you and Daisy actually do ANY spying at all?'

'Not *exactly*. OK – no. Sorry. We didn't do any.'

'WHAT? NOTHING?!' You could practically see steam coming out of Flora's ears.

'I'm sorry, Flora!' said Daisy, her eyes filling with tears. 'It's all my fault! I asked Wogan to teach me how to street dance and that's taken up all our time!'

'Wogan? Street dance? As in *this* Wogan?' Flora said, a very confused look on her face.

'Yes!' sniffed Daisy. 'He's been teaching me how to pop and lock. And some old-school b-boy steps . . . All the way up to more modern krumping.'

'Let me be totally clear,' said Flora. 'You're saying that *Wogan* can *street dance*?'

'Yes. His electric boogaloo has to be seen to be believed.'

'I'm sure. Wogan, why don't – Hang on, where did Wogan go?'

'Oh,' said Daisy. 'In return for my dance lessons, I've been teaching Wogan how to silently sneak in and out of places.'

'Unbelievable,' said Flora. 'Anyway, guys, we have work to do! We need to get into the basement AND Dylan's locker!'

'I think we need to move quickly as well,' said Charlie.

'Why's that?' asked Mohsen.

'Because of something Dylan said. He said that the school dance was going to be wild. I think that's when he's planning to do something.'

'In that case,' said Flora, 'we only have three days to stop him. Charlie – we're going to need you to do some changing!'

CHAPTER 9

'OK – so here's the plan,' Flora said to her three friends the next day. 'At break time, as soon as the bell goes, we make a diversion to get Dylan out of the room and make sure he forgets his bag. Then, Charlie, you try and turn into something small. If you turn into something like a mouse, hide in his bag, and poke your head out and see what Dylan's up to when he goes to his locker or the basement. If you turn into anything smaller, like a flea or something, you can just hop on to Dylan and spy from there.'

'OK, Captain!' Charlie said, smiling and giving a smart salute.

'Can I create the diversion?' asked Wogan, with his hand up.

'You sure can,' said Flora.

'It certainly sounds like an excellent plan, Flora,' said Mohsen. 'Completely foolproof.'

'That's right,' agreed Wogan. 'I can't see this going wrong at all. There's absolutely no way it will turn into a disaster and put Charlie in mortal danger.'

The moment the bell went, the friends sprang into action. Flora and Mohsen went to guard the door as the class flocked out. Meanwhile, Wogan walked up to Dylan and poked him in the chest.

'Oi – Van der Gruyne,' he said.

'What?' Dylan sneered.

Only at that moment did Wogan realize he hadn't yet thought how he was going to create the diversion he was supposed to be carrying out.

'I . . . err . . . I . . . errrrrr . . .'

'Come on!' snapped Dylan. 'I haven't got all day!'

'I . . . errrrrrrrrrrr . . . was . . . ermmmmm . . . wondering if you'd like to go to the school dance with me?'

'If I'd WHAT?' Dylan replied, a look of disbelief on his face.

'If you'd like to go to the school dance with me?' Wogan repeated, looking like he didn't quite believe the words coming out of his own mouth.

'No!' barked Dylan. 'I would not like to go to the school dance with you. In fact, I can't think of a single thing I'd less like to do.'

'Is it because you're a rubbish dancer?' asked Wogan gently. 'There's no need to be embarrassed if you are.'

'A what? How DARE you? No, I am NOT a rubbish dancer! I'm a better dancer than you! WHO told you I was rubbish?'

'Oh, you know, just people. But you don't have to prove anything to anyone.'

'I could prove it ANY time, you lanky wazzock!'

'Well, you *could* show me how good a dancer you are right now. In the playground. Unless you're too scared?'

'RIGHT! Come on!' shouted Dylan, standing up. 'Let's go! Right now! To the playground! DANCE-OFF!'

Dylan stormed out of the classroom and Wogan quickly followed, giving his friends two thumbs up behind Dylan's back.

Once they had both gone and the room was empty, Flora said, 'OK, Charlie, now's your chance! Think SMALL!'

Charlie sat on Dylan's desk so he wouldn't have far to travel if he did manage to turn small.

He closed his eyes and remembered the previous evening: his father forcing smiles and jokes while he packed his belongings in boxes and suitcases; Charlie trying not to cry in front of his dad and making it worse.

That was when the realization had really hit Charlie – his dad was actually moving out. Nothing was ever going to be the same again, and none of his family was even asking if *he* was OK because everybody was too wrapped up in their own problems.

As Charlie began to change, he had one word in his mind: tiny. Because that was how he felt when he saw all the huge problems in his life – like a tiny worm.

Charlie began shrinking fast, his legs and arms disappearing.

And he kept shrinking.

And he *kept* shrinking.

More.

And more.

Until he was tinier than he had ever been. Smaller than a fly. Smaller than a flea.

Charlie had changed, he realized, into a tiny, TINY worm.[24]

Two thoughts hit Charlie in quick succession. The first was a burst of delight – he was closer than ever to being able to choose what creature he changed into!

Before, he had just tried picturing what the animal looked like but that hadn't worked – he needed to *feel* how that animal felt. If he wanted to change into a gazelle, he couldn't just think of a gazelle – he needed to imagine what it was like *being* a gazelle, running across the vast plains of the Serengeti, scanning the horizon for deadly

---

[24] Charlie was a nematode worm. Nematodes are one of the most interesting creatures in existence. They are tiny, thread-like creatures, and can lay as many as 200,000 eggs in a single day. Imagine a chicken laying 200,000 eggs in a day. You might never even have heard of nematodes, but here's something remarkable – they account for eighty per cent of all animals on Earth! That's right: EIGHTY PER CENT OF ALL ANIMALS ON OUR PLANET ARE NEMATODES.

lions. If he wanted to change into a bird, he couldn't just think of an eagle or a magpie – he needed to feel the wind beneath his wings, his feathers ruffling silently as he glided, cradled by a current of air. Charlie had finally cracked it, he was sure.

The second thought that hit Charlie was that he was in BIG, **BIG** trouble. Or, more accurately, tiny, tiny trouble. When he had changed, he had been sitting on Dylan's desk. But now he was *so* tiny, the cracks and bumps on the plastic surface looked like chasms and hills.[25] He glanced up but the size of everything, including his friends, made him dizzy.

---

[25] Nematodes don't actually have eyes, so although they are sensitive to light, they can't actually see. So how come Charlie has eyes and can see? And also – he doesn't have ears, so how can he hear? That's an excellent question, which has two possible answers:

1. When Charlie changed he managed to keep his eyes and ears or

2. I am choosing to ignore the biology of nematodes a tiny bit because I need Charlie to be able to see during this next bit of the story and I couldn't think of a way around it.

You can decide which answer to believe.

'Where's Charlie?' he heard Flora ask in panic. 'He's completely disappeared!'

'He must be so small we can't see him!' cried Mohsen. 'Be careful you don't tread on him!'

I'm right here, thought Charlie. *On Dylan's desk! I must be really tiny if they can't see me sitting here.*

Charlie knew that he was never going to be able to reach Dylan's bag, which was on the floor beside the desk – you might as well have asked him to fly to the sun and back. And there was no way he had time to change back into Charlie and then into another creature before Dylan made it back. How long could a dance-off last anyway? Probably not long enough, especially if Wogan was involved.

Charlie had to think, and think fast. He looked around the enormous desk. The only thing on it was a vast green apple. It was Dylan's break-time snack and, to worm-Charlie, it looked the size of a small moon.

It was his only hope.

If he could crawl over to the apple and cling on to it, maybe – just maybe – Dylan would pick it up and put it in his bag, and then . . . well, Charlie would have to think of what to do next when it came to it.

Charlie began wriggling, squeezing his little wormy body up and down like a tiny accordion. Slowly, he made his way across the desk, going around the bigger cracks, the apple getting larger and larger as he got nearer and nearer.

He could hear Flora and Mohsen still looking for him as he arrived at the bottom of the apple and began climbing up.

And it wasn't a moment too soon, as Dylan burst back into the classroom, muttering furiously to himself.

'I can't believe it! How on earth did that dimwit know the electric boogaloo? Unbelievable. What are you losers gawping at anyway?'

'Nothing!' replied Flora.

'None of your business!' replied Mohsen.

'Where's Charlie, the king of the losers?' sneered Dylan, as Wogan came in behind him.

'He's not the king of the losers!' shouted Mohsen.

'Yeah!' said Wogan. 'We're all equal!'

Dylan gave a high-pitched laugh. 'Whatever you say, equal losers.'

He grabbed his apple.

Yes, thought Charlie, as Dylan's humongous hand swept him into the air. *It's working! Looks like my luck is turning for the better at last!*

If you've been following Charlie's adventures

for a while, you know he has quite a lot of experience of being completely and totally wrong.

Well, this was a new record in wrongness.[26] Charlie was spectacularly, extraordinarily, mind-bogglingly, pants-wettingly, universe-banjaxingly wrong.

Or, to put it another way, Charlie's luck was not turning for the better, but turning for the worse.

The much, MUCH, MUCH, MUCH, **MUCH, MUCH** worse.

Because Dylan didn't put the apple in his bag.

Oh no.

He started eating it.

The first bite sent Charlie into a frenzy of absolute terror as Dylan's vast mouth widened above him like a wet, pink cave, towering teeth

[26] I'm talking Guinness World Records level of wrongness.

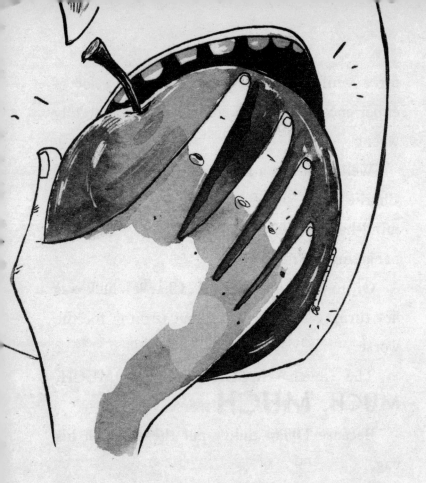

glistening, tongue curling like a pale, beached whale.

Charlie crawled as fast as he could, desperately trying to get to the bottom of the apple, where the underside would afford him some safety.

The mouth chomped on the apple a second time, the teeth coming even closer, the sound of the crunching bite deafening. Charlie had faced murderous cats and nearly been munched by hungry crocodiles but he had never experienced anything like the terror he felt at the sight of Dylan's slavering mouth.

The second bite had missed him – but only just.

And as Dylan came in for a third, Charlie realized there was nothing he could do. The mouth was coming his way. His fate was sealed.

This was how Charlie McGuffin was going to meet his end – eaten by Dylan van der Gruyne.

If Charlie could have screamed, he would have done.[27]

Then the mouth closed around him and everything went black.

---

[27] He couldn't because nematode worms can't scream. Which is why it's good to sit next to them on roller coasters if you have really sensitive ears.

CHAPTER 10

As Dylan's gnashing teeth closed, there was only one way for Charlie to go: further into Dylan's mouth. Dropping off the apple, he landed on Dylan's tongue.

It was like riding a fleshy wave – the tongue was rippling and thrashing, throwing Charlie all over the place. Saliva gushed around him in a sticky rushing tide. Chunks of apple battered and buffeted Charlie as he clung on for dear life but finally a big lump smacked him squarely in his worm-face, knocking him clean off the tongue in a swirling spiral of saliva.

Blind terror clutched at Charlie as he was pulled – no, *swallowed* – down Dylan's throat.

He desperately tried to swim back up but it was impossible; he was caught in a great surging current of saliva and apple bits, while the muscly tube of flesh[28] surrounding him was squeezing and contracting, creating unstoppable waves. Down he was squeezed, down he was pulled, and down he was washed in a dark, rolling tide.

And Charlie knew where he was heading. He had paid enough attention in science lessons to know that at the end of this journey was the stomach.

And the stomach was full of acid.

And that was how he was going to die – dissolved into nothing in Dylan's stomach.

Unless . . .

No.

He couldn't.

Could he?

---

[28] Otherwise known as the 'oesophagus'. Or 'esophagus' if you are American. Americans often spell things ~~incorrectly~~ differently from British people.

Maybe . . . if . . . if he changed back into a boy right now, Charlie might just survive.

But Dylan definitely wouldn't.

If Charlie changed while he was still inside Dylan . . . Well, the less said about *that* the better, but rest assured Dylan would most definitely have a very, VERY sticky end.

And with a sinking feeling, Charlie realized he could never, ever do that, not even to his mortal enemy. He had no choice but to accept his acidy fate.

Charlie's eyes had become accustomed enough to the dark to see he was approaching a fleshy valve, flapping open and closed.

It was the entrance to the stomach.

Charlie stopped struggling and allowed himself to be dragged down to his doom. The great valve snapped open and Charlie landed with a tiny plop in the soup of acidy stomach juices and semi-digested food.

He waited for the burning, agonizing death. But it didn't come. Instead . . .

'Morning!' came a cheery voice.

'Morning!' came another, equally cheery, voice.

'Hello! New down here, are you?' came yet another cheery voice.

Voices? That I can understand? That can only mean one thing, Charlie thought. *There must be more worms in here!*

'Hello!' Charlie called back. 'So worms can survive in stomach acid, can they?'

'Oh yes!' called back another worm. 'It's lovely! Like a warm bath!'

Charlie had to agree – it was exactly like swimming in a warm bath. Not at all what he'd expected. Slowly, Charlie began to be able to make out the pale wriggling shapes of other worms. *Lots* of other worms.

'So how many of you are down here?' Charlie asked.

'Well, including you, ninety-seven thousand, four hundred and twenty-six,' replied a worm.

'No,' replied another worm. 'You're still counting Delbert 237. He died.'

'Oh! You're quite right. Poor old Delbert 237. So that means you're number ninety-seven thousand, four hundred and twenty-*five*.'

Charlie couldn't quite believe how many worms there were in Dylan's stomach.[29]

'What's your name?' a worm called out.

---

[29] In fact, nematode worms are *everywhere*. Half of all people in the world have them in their stomachs. But not just that, they are found in every part of the planet, from the coldest to the hottest place, from the bottom of the ocean to the sand in the desert. They are in soil and plants and trees and almost all animals. They are EVERYWHERE.

'Charlie,' replied Charlie.

'Oh, that makes you Charlie 1921!'

'There are 1,920 other worms down here called Charlie?' asked Charlie in amazement.

Before any worms could answer though, the walls of Dylan's stomach suddenly contracted, creating huge waves in the juices. All the worms whooped and cheered, and Charlie had to admit that it did remind him of swimming in the local pool when the wave machine was turned on. Only the excited yells of the worms gave it more of a party feel.

'Come on, Charlie! Swim with us!'

Charlie started swimming in the waves, and realized he was rather enjoying himself.

But deep down, he knew he couldn't stay.

He had to somehow get back to his friends.

'Does anybody know how to get out of here?'

'Get out?!' exclaimed one worm. 'Why would you want to do that? Stay!'

'That's right!' called another worm. 'Stay!'

'Stay!' all the worms started shouting. 'Stay and play!'

Playing didn't sound half bad to Charlie. Maybe it would be OK to stay just a *bit* longer . . .

No, Charlie thought, trying to snap himself out of it. *I can't forget who I am!*

'I can't! I have to go!'

'Oh what a party-pooper!'

'Yes! What a spoilsport!'

'Maybe we shouldn't tell you the way out!'

'No, don't tell him! Stay down here and play with us! Come play with us, Charlie . . . forever!'

'And ever!'

'And ever!'

Charlie was beginning to realize that the worms were going to be no help. He was going to have to find his own way out.

Charlie thought back to the plastic model of the human body that he'd been given for his birthday a couple of years ago. The way out of the stomach was the intestine! That long, twisting tunnel was his escape route. He just had to find the opening.

It has to be down, thought Charlie, so he began swimming down, through the bubbling sludge.

'Don't go!' shouted the worms. 'Stay!'

'We'll have such fun! Stay with us, Charlie!'

'Stay!'

'Staaaay . . . Plaaay . . .'

But their voices soon faded, drowned out by the gurgling of stomach juices as Charlie swam away from the

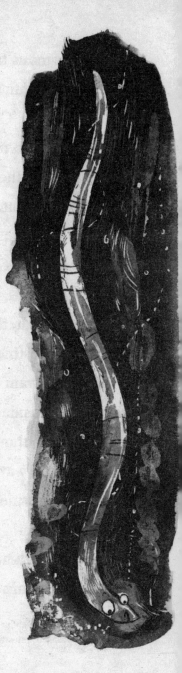

creepy worms as fast he could, searching for the opening to Dylan's intestine.

As he swam, Charlie noticed a gentle current pulling him down, like you get in a bath when you pull out the plug. He swam down the spiralling current, praying that it was his way out.

There it is! Charlie thought, excitedly. *A tunnel!*

Sure enough, there it was: the opening which led to the intestine.

Charlie swam through, a tiny bud of hope blossoming inside him.

But even though he was hopeful, Charlie knew he had a way to go. He didn't know exactly how long intestines were, but he knew they were *very* long.[30]

And at the other end of the intestine was . . . well, Charlie didn't want to think about *that* yet.

[30] A child's intestine is about six metres long. That's about the length of two three-metre pieces of intestine! Or six one-metre pieces of intestine.

On Charlie swam. The intestines squeezed, just like the oesophagus and stomach had done, helping to push him along. He met the odd worm, desperately trying to swim back towards the stomach. They weren't having much luck though, swimming against the current.

'What are you doing?' the worms called out to Charlie, as he swam past. 'You'll die if you go that way! Come back!'

But Charlie had no intention of going back to the stomach. He had to escape. He had to get out and see his friends again.

And as he swam down the intestine, Charlie realized something. It was definitely his friends he most wanted to see again – not his mum and dad. Because he was angry with his parents. Furious. *Furious* for ruining his life. *Why* did they have to separate? How could they do this to him?

On Charlie swam, propelled by his fury. He

wanted to get out of here and scream at his mum and dad.

Scream at them – and then hug them. And let the tears come.

There were small brown lumps in the liquid Charlie was swimming through now, and the lumps were getting bigger.

Charlie had been doing his best to ignore them but, deep down, he knew what they were.

It was time to face up to the truth.

The brown lumps were poo.

The exit he was travelling towards was Dylan's bum.

And Dylan's bum was Charlie's only chance of survival.

But he had to do it – he had to swim on. He had no choice. Charlie wanted to live.

So he beat on, worming along the current, borne forward ceaselessly into the poo.

The poo was becoming more frequent now, huge boulders of it, and the current had stopped, so Charlie had to start wriggling.

Just when he thought he could take no more, Charlie saw an opening – a light at the end of the tunnel.

But then, from far behind, way back along the intestine, came a distant rumbling sound. It grew louder and louder, until suddenly a blast of foul air swept over Charlie, rocketing him forward in a rasping, noxious cloud, straight out of the opening and face-first into a soft cloth barrier.

I've made it! Charlie thought. *I've reached Dylan's underpants! I'm saved!*

And Charlie felt such a surge of relief and happiness that two things happened at once.

- From Charlie's perspective, he felt a flash of tingling electricity, flew through the air and by the time he landed on the floor of the boys' changing room, he was back to plain old Charlie again.

- From Dylan's perspective, he was in the boys' changing room, minding his own business, when he did a tiny little fart and Charlie McGuffin exploded out of his bum.

Charlie lay on the floor, panting, glad to be alive.

Dylan stood on the other side of the room, the back of his pants and trousers ripped clean off – again.

'What did you . . .? How did you . . .? Where did you . . .?' he burbled.

'Don't ask, Dylan,' Charlie said, standing up and brushing himself down. 'It's best neither of us mentions this ever again. To anyone. Agreed?'

'I . . . But . . .' stammered Dylan, clutching his bum. 'I . . . Agreed. My mum's only just mended these trousers! You'll pay for them, McGuffin!'

Charlie suddenly noticed that Dylan was standing next to his locker.

And his locker was wide open.

And inside the locker was a furry costume.

A furry *bear* costume.

Oh my goodness! Charlie thought. *It* is *Dylan that's pretending to be animals!*

Dylan slammed the locker shut and walked to the door, but Charlie blocked his way.

'I know what you're up to, Dylan,' Charlie said.

'Oh DO you?' asked Dylan, the cruel smirk returning to his face despite him trying to hold his trousers together and hide his bum.

'Yeah. I do. You've been dressing up in that bear costume in your locker and kidnapping animals all over town. You're trying to make people think it's me.'

Dylan sniffed. 'Very clever, McGuffin. You're not nearly as stupid as you look.'

'Yeah, whatever. So, I've just got one question for you.'

'What's that?'

'What have you done with the Great Catsby?'

'The Great *What*-sby?'

'My cat!'

'I haven't got your stupid cat!'

'Oh, come on! Don't try and deny it. I want my cat back!'

'I have no idea what has happened to your flea-ridden cat. And McGuffin?'

'What?'

'You absolutely STINK.'

Before Charlie could say another word, a few Year 3 boys bustled into the changing room. Dylan took the opportunity to squeeze past him and strutted off, holding his nose, leaving Charlie stood in the changing room, his head a jumble of thoughts.

CHAPTER 11

It was one day until the school dance, two days until his father was going to move out and Charlie had a LOT of explaining to do to his friends.

'OK,' said Wogan. 'Let's go through this one more time. You turned into a tiny worm and you *jumped* on to Dylan? And then you saw him open his locker?'

'That's right,' said Charlie, licking his dry lips.

'Exactly how small were you?' asked Mohsen. 'You must have been absolutely tiny for us not to be able to see you.'

'Yeah, I was really teeny-tiny,' said Charlie.

'So how did you jump on to Dylan? Because worms really can't jump very far. At all. *Especially* not teeny-tiny ones.'

'I . . . erm . . . Well, I . . . erm . . .'

'He's erming, Wogan,' said Mohsen, eyeing Charlie. 'Some seriously suspicious erming there.'

'I told you what happened,' said Charlie, crossing his arms. 'If you don't want to believe me . . .'

'We *want* to believe you,' said Wogan. 'I just think your story has more holes than my favourite underpants.'

Mohsen shuddered. 'Ugh, yes, those pants do have a *lot* of holes. You should really think about throwing them away.'

'Fine! Don't believe me!' growled Charlie.

'We do, Charlie! We do! Anyway,' said Flora, desperately changing the subject, 'isn't it great you can finally control what animal you change into!'

'I guess so . . . I mean, I *think* I've cracked it, although –'

'Because, you know, you wanted to change into something tiny, and then – hey presto! – you turned into a mysterious, invisible jumping worm,' added Mohsen.

'Yes,' said Charlie, glaring at Mohsen.

'Are you *sure* you're telling us *everything*?' Flora said, looking concerned. 'You know you don't have to keep secrets from us. It's better to share –'

'I *can't*,' said Charlie in a small voice.

'You can!'

'I can't,' Charlie said with an air of finality.

'Oh come on! It can't be as bad as being dropped in a bath of Wogan's wee!' said Mohsen.

'It's worse. It's actually the worst thing possible.'

'Worst thing *possible*?' said Wogan. 'No way. It's not like Dylan accidentally ate you and farted you out! Now *that* would be the worst thing possible.'

Charlie made a strangled noise of shock.

'**HOLYYYY MACKEREL!**' gasped Wogan, mouth flapping, fish-like. 'That's what happened, isn't it?'

Charlie looked at the floor, his face bright red. He didn't reply. He wanted the ground to swallow him.

'That is actually, **ACTUALLY** the most amazing thing I have ever heard. You're the first person *ever* to go inside a human body! Wow!' Wogan slapped Charlie on the back. 'Charlie McGuffin, you are the most awesome person in the world!'

Charlie let out a shy smile. Suddenly he didn't want the ground to swallow him. Suddenly he felt quite proud and lucky to have such good friends. He felt tears of happiness prickling in his eyes.

'So Dylan had a bear costume in his locker?' said Mohsen quickly. 'He's always up to no good!'

Charlie nodded. 'Yup.'

'Now we have proof it's definitely him pretending to be animals. He is trying to set you up, to make it look like you're eating them. But *why* is he keeping them in the basement and *what* is he going to do at the school dance?' asked Flora, her brow furrowed.

Charlie's heart ached at the thought of the Great Catsby, trapped in the basement, so close to him.

'Why don't we just tell the teachers?' he asked.

Flora shook her head. 'Dylan would just deny he put the animals down there and we'd get the blame.'

'Get the blame for what?' asked Daisy suddenly from behind the four friends.

'ARGH!' yelped Flora in surprise, spinning to face Daisy and Lola. 'How do you two keep doing that? You're so silent!'

Charlie quickly explained what he'd discovered to Daisy and Lola.

'So we have one day to get the key off Dylan and the animals out of the basement before he carries out his plan!' Flora added.

'OK!' said Daisy. 'That's all great and super-interesting and everything, but I was actually just here to ask if Wogan would go to the dance with me?'

Flora buried her face in her hands and groaned.

'I'm confused now,' said Wogan. 'I thought you'd already asked me and –'

'YES OR NO?' snapped Daisy.

'Yes,' nodded Wogan, his look of terror badly disguised behind a smile.

'Great!' said Daisy. 'Do you and Moh want to practise dance moves in the playground?'

'We can't,' said Wogan glumly. 'We have to find a way into the basement!'

'It's OK, you go!' said Charlie, a smile on his face. 'Flora and I will get our thinking caps on and try to work out how to get the key from Dylan.'

Mohsen and Wogan walked out, chattering to Lola and Daisy, leaving Charlie and Flora alone.

A moment of weighty silence stretched out between them.

'So . . . Flor . . . I was wondering –' Charlie began, before Flora interrupted him.

'Charlie, would you go to the dance with me?'

Charlie tried playing it cool but he couldn't help his beaming smile. 'I was just about to ask you – yes! Yes, I would. Definitely.'

'Great!' Flora returned Charlie's smile with a grin just as big.

'Great!' replied Charlie, still smiling from ear to ear.

Charlie's smile lasted through doublemaths and geography, all the way until the end of the school day, right up until he bumped into Dylan on the way home.

They squared up to each other.

'Looking forward to the dance tomorrow, McGuffin?'

'Get lost, Dylan. I know you're up to something. But we'll stop you,' said Charlie.

'Stop me? You don't even know what I'm planning!' Dylan scoffed.

'Well, isn't this the moment you reveal your plan and tell me there's nothing I can do about it?'

'Oh no, McGuffin. I'm not telling you a *thing*.'

'You call yourself a proper villain? Villains always reveal their plan to gloat! And you're a gloater.'

'You really believe I'm that stupid, McGuffin?' Dylan said. Thinking for a moment, he continued, 'I will tell you *one* thing though. Guess who recorded you turning into a fly the other day? That's right. Me! And guess who's going to show the video to the whole school on the big screen at the dance tomorrow? Me! And then guess who's going to remind everybody about all the missing animals? Right again! Me! And then who will everyone think ate all those animals? *You!* Freaky, animal-changing Charlie McGuffin!'

'That actually sounds like your whole plan you just told me there,' Charlie said.

'GAH!' exclaimed Dylan, slapping his forehead. 'Blast it! Never mind. It won't stop anything. The whole town will hate you. Almost as much as I do.'

'Why are you like this, Dylan? Why do you hate me *so* much?'

Dylan looked Charlie in the eye for a long moment. Then he replied in a quiet voice.

'You really don't remember, do you?'

'No, I don't.'

'Why doesn't that surprise me?' Dylan said flatly.

'Dylan, what are you talking about?'

'Right,' said Dylan. 'Looks like we need a flashback to remind you. Brace yourself . . .'

It was the first day of Year 2 and Dylan van der Gruyne's first day at his new school. He was feeling pretty nervous. All the other children seemed to know each other and were chatting excitedly to their friends. Dylan sat quietly, his ears glowing with embarrassment.

The teacher finally shushed the class and introduced Dylan. He could feel himself blushing hard as the teacher asked a boy called Charlie McGuffin to be his 'Class Buddy' for the next two weeks to help him settle in. But when Dylan turned to look at Charlie, he gave him a nice smile, which made him feel loads better.

Dylan and Charlie quickly became firm friends. For the next few days, they played together all the time and that made it a lot easier for Dylan to feel accepted. Dylan even came over to Charlie's house on a play date. They built a den in Charlie's bedroom, then had pizza for tea.

For the first time in a long time, Dylan was happy.

And then it all went wrong.

It was the Great Snail Race that did it. All the children had been training their snails, feeding them snaffled bits of icky wet lettuce and cucumber. Every day they smuggled them into school in takeaway boxes with holes punched in the lids. The children raced the snails every lunchtime at the far corner of the playground, cheering on their favourite.

After a complex series of group stages, knockout rounds, quarter-finals and semi-finals, the grand final had at last arrived.

The four finalists were:

- Charlie McGuffin and his snail *BLUE THUNDER*
- Dylan van der Gruyne and *SEVERUS SNAIL*
- Iris Murdoch from 2P and her snail *THE BLACK PRINCE*
- Teddy Gruber and *POO-HEAD SNAIL-FACE THE THIRD*

Tension rippled through the crowd as the four children placed their racing snails on the starting line.

'Get set!' shouted the race commentator, a small boy from 3H.

'Five!'

'Four!'

The crowd surged forward, eager to get the best view.

'Three!'

'Two!'

The surging crowd knocked into Charlie, who was squatting on his haunches, sending him sprawling. As Charlie fell forward across the starting line, he felt a sickening crunch under his face.

'Ugh!' Charlie jumped up, wiping his face. 'I squashed a snail! Yech!' Sure enough, Charlie had bits of shell and gloopy blobs of snail dripping off his cheek.

'SEVERUS!' Dylan cried. 'YOU SMASHED SEVERUS!'

Silence fell over the crowd.

'YOU DID THAT ON PURPOSE!' Dylan shouted. 'YOU KNEW MY SNAIL WAS GOING TO WIN AND YOU SQUASHED HIM!'

Charlie stood in shock, not able to get his words out, crushed snail sliding down his face.

'I-I-I . . .' Charlie stammered.

A ripple of nervous laughter ran through the crowd.

Charlie couldn't help it – it was everybody else laughing that did it. A small smile crept on to his face as he wiped his cheek with his sleeve.

And Dylan saw that smile.

And that smile made tears spring into Dylan's eyes.

And the other children saw Dylan start crying and started laughing harder.

Dylan took one last look at Charlie, who was trying to stifle his smile.

'I didn't mean –' Charlie started.

But Dylan didn't wait to hear. He turned and started walking away as fast as he could, hot tears rolling down his cheeks, laughter ringing in his ears.

And that was the end of the friendship between Dylan van der Gruyne and Charlie McGuffin.

'That's it?!' Charlie exclaimed. 'That's the reason you've hated me all these years? I didn't mean to squash your snail! It was a complete accident!'

Dylan stared Charlie down.

'You just don't get it, do you, McGuffin? Maybe it wasn't your fault. But you don't remember what it was like. For weeks afterwards, everyone laughed at me. And you ignored me.'

'I didn't! I tried saying sorry and you stormed off.'

'I was angry! And sad. And lonely. You tried saying sorry to me once. And then you never spoke to me again.'

'I thought you didn't want to be friends with me any more,' said Charlie quietly.

'I did,' said Dylan. 'But you didn't even try.'

Charlie was beginning to feel very bad

indeed. 'I'm sorry,' he said quietly.

'Thanks. But it's too late.'

'What? Why?'

'Our story began on that day, McGuffin. And it finishes tomorrow. Severus Snail will finally get his revenge at the school dance.'

CHAPTER 12

Charlie slept fitfully that night – his dreams full of trapped cats and squashed snails – and when the day of the school dance finally arrived, he couldn't have felt less like celebrating or dancing. He was exhausted. The recollection that the Great Catsby was still missing hit Charlie like a punch and the house felt deathly quiet as he ate his soggy cornflakes, as if sadness had sucked all the air out of it. Charlie felt he could hardly breathe.

His dad was moving out tomorrow.

It was their last day living together as a family.

It was actually happening.

SmoothMove walked into the kitchen carrying an empty breakfast bowl, which he chucked into the dishwasher. He looked at Charlie, who looked mournfully back at him.

'It sucks, right?' said SmoothMove.

Charlie nodded.

'It doesn't mean they love us any less, though, you know.'

Charlie stared into his cereal. He could feel tears starting.

SmoothMove came over and ruffled Charlie's hair. 'And we've always got each other.'

And then Charlie cried.

SmoothMove put a comforting arm round Charlie, and Charlie swung round and buried himself into SmoothMove's chest and sobbed, long and hard. SmoothMove held him tightly, letting his pyjamas get soaked with his brother's tears.

'It's not fair!' Charlie wept. 'It's not fair!'

'You're right,' said SmoothMove. 'It's totally not fair. It's life, though. And we always get through these tough times and out the other side.'

Charlie stopped crying and felt a bit better. He smiled at SmoothMove and felt a little burst of bravery swell in his chest.

'Now, wipe your eyes and get ready for school,' SmoothMove said. 'You've got your school dance tonight, right?'

'Yup!' said Charlie, and then, very quickly, whilst he gobbled his cereal, he filled in his brother on everything that had been going on with the missing pets and Dylan trying to frame him.

'And,' he added, 'Flora asked me to go to the dance with her. But I don't know how to dance!' Charlie grimaced. 'Wogan said he would teach me how to do some basic toprocks, possibly even the windmill and headspin, but I don't reckon we'll have time today, what with trying to get the key to the basement from Dylan and whatnot. So on top of everything else, I'm going to embarrass myself in front of Flora tonight.'

'Charlie,' said SmoothMove. 'Let me give you some advice. You don't need to breakdance to impress Flora. She likes you for who you are. Just enjoy yourself – have fun, do whatever – *that's* the best way to dance.'

'Thanks, SmoothMove. You know, you're all right – for a smelly big brother!'

Charlie grinned and ran upstairs to get ready for school.

★★★

The day seemed to disappear in a blur, and no matter what Charlie and his friends did, they couldn't get the key from Dylan.

At first break, Charlie changed into a tiny mouse and climbed up Dylan's trouser leg to get the key out of his pocket, while Flora tried to distract Dylan by asking if he wanted to go to the dance with her. But Dylan had felt mouse-Charlie and screamed, so Charlie had to run away without being seen.

At lunch, Wogan tried bamboozling Dylan by doing headspins while Mohsen sneaked up on him from behind and picked his pocket. But

OW!

Mohsen got his hand stuck, and Dylan turned round and poked him in the eye.

By the end of the day, the four friends were in despair.

'It's hopeless,' said Charlie, his face like a wet Wednesday. 'I really am finished. There's nothing we can do to stop Dylan this time. All the stolen animals are still missing and he's got the video of me changing, so all the evidence points to me. The whole town is going to think I'm a freak who's been going around eating their pets.'

'Maybe we could get his phone off him?' said Mohsen. 'Then he wouldn't have anything to show on the big screen?'

'No,' replied Charlie, forlornly. 'He'll have a backup. It's pointless.'

'Maybe we could just smash our way into the basement?' suggested Wogan.

'We can't do that either,' said Charlie. 'Mr O'Dear's office is just down the corridor, so he'd hear us and we'd totally get in trouble for damaging school property.'

'So we're back to square one then.'

'I have another idea,' said Flora. 'But it's risky.'

'Go on,' said Charlie.

'We kidnap Dylan, force him to open the basement and then lock him in there until the dance is over. I know it's extreme,' Flora continued, 'but if we can prove the animals are alive AND stop Dylan showing the video this evening, Charlie will be OK.'

'Dylan could still upload the video on the internet,' Mohsen pointed out.

'But once the stolen animals are all back, people will just think it's fake. No one's stupid enough to believe something like that on the internet.'

The boys all nodded.

'We're agreed then?'

'Definitely,' said Charlie with grim determination.

'In that case,' said Flora, 'here's the plan . . .'

★★★

That evening, the four friends arrived at the dance early.

The hall had been totally transformed. Lights and lasers were beaming across the room, which now looked like a dance floor. Streamers, which the Reception children had spent the last week making, hung from the ceiling and walls. Music blared from the speakers at the far end of the hall, where a local DJ was shouting something unintelligible into a microphone.

Slowly, the hall began to fill up with excited children. Half an hour later, it was practically full. It seemed the whole year was there – except Dylan.

Lola and Daisy came up and asked Wogan and Mohsen if they wanted to dance. Wogan began wildly breakdancing whilst nervously glancing around, looking for Dylan. Mohsen began nervously breakdancing whilst wildly glancing around, looking for Dylan. Flora and Charlie nervously glanced at Mohsen's attempts to breakdance.

Finally, Dylan arrived. He was alone, as usual, and stood in the corner of the hall, looking scornfully at all the other children dancing.

Flora nudged Charlie. 'Now's our chance.'

Wogan and Mohsen had also seen Dylan arrive and nodded at each other.

It was time to put Flora's plan into action.

The first step was simple: Mohsen and Wogan had to get to the basement.

Unfortunately, the plan broke down at this very first simple step.

Maybe it was the swirling lights and music that made Wogan completely forget what he was meant to do. Maybe it was Daisy whispering in his ear. We will never know. But instead of following the very simple plan, Wogan ran straight over to Dylan and started popping and locking, right in Dylan's face.

The crowd parted.

It was a dance-off!

Dylan started with some basic moves, a bit of crowd-hyping followed by robot dancing, and then dropped down into a head slide.

The crowd gasped.

Wogan replied with a classic windmill, and then snapped into a particularly sick jack-hammer.

'What on earth are they *doing*?' Charlie shouted into Flora's ear.

'I have absolutely no idea,' Flora shouted in reply, shaking her head. 'It looks like they're getting electric shocks.'

Dylan, meanwhile, was pulling some sweet air-flares and then went straight into a tight headspin.

The crowd was whooping and cheering.

After a few more minutes of what seemed like never-ending breakdancing moves, Flora lost her temper.

'Oh, for goodness' sake! I can't take any

more of their ridiculous flailing.'

She stormed towards the dancing pair. Wogan saw the look on Flora's face and suddenly remembered the plan. He ran off in the direction of the basement, closely followed by Mohsen.

The crowd groaned.

'Ha!' cried Dylan, raising his fists above his head. 'Victory is mine!'

Charlie and Flora sauntered up, trying very hard to look innocent.

'Why are you two trying so hard to look innocent?' sneered Dylan.

'We're not!' said Charlie.

'That's a good job because you'd be failing miserably if you were. What do you two nincompoops want?'

'We don't *want* anything,' said Flora. 'We just have to tell you that Mr O'Dear is looking for you. He said something about knowing what's going on in the basement?'

Dylan turned ghostly white and his mouth flopped open.

'Well, go on!' shouted Flora. 'You'd best go and find him.'

Dylan looked in panic from Charlie to Flora and then bolted – also in the direction of the basement.

Charlie high-fived Flora.

'I can't believe he fell for that so easily!'

'Me neither,' grinned Flora. 'Come on!'

Charlie and Flora ran after Dylan down the empty corridors of the school, disco music echoing faintly behind them. But while Flora kept running, Charlie dodged into the boys' toilet.

He checked the toilet stalls were empty, then closed his eyes and began to change. It had never been easier to tap into his negative thoughts. His family was splitting up tomorrow. That was the only thought Charlie needed. His life ahead was filled with uncertainty. His body flooded with fear and worry and sorrow.

As he felt the electricity surge through his body, Charlie thought of the fiercest animal he knew – a lion. But he didn't just picture it; he imagined the beast prowling across the savannah as the sun set; he felt the warm wind softly ruffling his mane, carrying the teasing scent of gazelle, the crunch of dry grass under his heavy paws. And the feeling it gave him: no fear, just an animal at peace, under an endless, darkening blue sky, the last strokes of pale pink slowly disappearing and the horizon stretching forever ahead of him.

Charlie was growing, his arms turning into legs, his hands and feet into paws. He could feel fur springing up all over his body, his teeth and nails sharpening.

This time, there was no doubt in his mind

and, a moment later, a glance in the mirror confirmed it – Charlie was a lion.

Charlie could finally choose what animal to turn into.

He could choose when to change and when to change back.

Charlie could finally completely control his power.

He had never felt more like a superhero.

CHAPTER 13

Charlie pawed his way through the bathroom door and sprang down the corridor. When he turned the corner, there they all were, as planned: Flora, Wogan, Mohsen and, in the middle of them, pinned against the basement door, was Dylan.

Charlie was pleased to see that, even though they knew he was coming, his friends still all did a leap of fright when they saw him. It was human instinct – if you see a huge lion pad towards you, you fear for your life.

Charlie strode up to Dylan, jumped up on his hind legs, and placed his front paws either side of Dylan's head. He breathed heavily on

Dylan's face, a low rumbling growl, deep in his throat, which seemed to shake the air.

Dylan whimpered and slipped to the floor.

'I . . . know . . . that's you . . . Charlie!' Dylan snivelled. 'You won't do anything to me. You wouldn't dare!'

Flora kneeled down and spoke quietly to Dylan.

'We thought you'd say that. But you need to understand – you've made Charlie desperate. He's willing to do anything. And if that means . . .'

Flora left the threat hanging but, to emphasise the point, Charlie widened his jaws over Dylan's face, letting hot drool drip down into his gibbering mouth. Dylan squirmed

backwards, desperate to get away from the glistening teeth.

'OK!' he whimpered. 'OK! You can have the key!'

Dylan reached into his pocket, but then his face went even paler, if that was possible. He checked his other pocket, panicking.

'It's gone!' he said. 'The key! It's gone!'

'CHILDREN!' came a sudden scream from the far end of the corridor. It was Mr Wind, his face a red explosion. 'GET AWAY FROM THAT LION!'

Instead of getting away from that lion, which would be the perfectly normal course of action, Mohsen, Flora and Wogan all groaned and slapped their foreheads.[31]

'Argh! Not now!' gasped Flora. 'Go away, Mr Wind!'

'SAVE YOURSELVES!' Mr Wind cried, bravely charging forward.

Flora, Mohsen, Wogan and Charlie the lion all froze in horror. Dylan saw his moment. He sprang up and sprinted away as fast as his terrified jelly legs would carry him, leaving the friends' plans in tatters.

'RUN, CHILDREN! What's wrong with you! For the love of all that's holy, WHY WON'T YOU RUN?!' cried Mr Wind.

Inspiration suddenly hit Wogan like a dozen hamsters dropped out of a plane without parachutes.

[31] Their own foreheads, not each other's. Just to be clear.

'Don't worry, sir!' he said, patting Charlie the lion. 'It's fine! This is my pet.'

Wogan, Flora and Charlie the lion turned in unison to Wogan, in total disbelief. This had to be Wogan's most ludicrous, doomed-to-fail idea ever. And there was some stiff competition for *that* title.

'He's harmless,' Wogan continued, ruffling Charlie's mane, ignoring the nagging voice in the back of his head telling him that this was his most ludicrous and doomed-to-fail idea yet. 'Perfectly safe.'

Mr Wind paused, panting, his face getting redder and redder.

'PERFECTLY SAFE?! WHAT ARE YOU THINKING? It was just attacking Van der Gruyne!'

'No he wasn't!' replied Wogan. 'We were just playing a game.'

'It didn't look like a game to me. The boy

was practically wetting himself.'

'It was a game! With my pet lion,' Wogan said with certainty.

Mr Wind eyeballed Wogan suspiciously.

Flora and Mohsen and Charlie waited for Mr Wind to explode.

'You have a pet lion?' Mr Wind asked.

'That's right, sir,' nodded Wogan innocently.

'A *pet* lion? As in, a *lion* that you have as an actual *pet*?'

Wogan simply nodded again, seemingly oblivious to the volcano that was about to erupt.

'And you thought you'd bring your *pet lion* into *my school*?'

'Yes, sir.'

'You thought you'd bring a pet lion into my school *on the day of the school dance*?'

'Yes, sir. I thought he'd enjoy the music.'

'YOU THOUGHT HE'D ENJOY THE MUSIC?' Mr Wind exploded. He practically had steam coming out of his ears. 'ARE YOU INSANE, BOY?'

The lion gave a look to Mr Wind, which if Mr Wind was not mistaken said, 'Yes. Wogan is completely insane.' Mr Wind shook his head, convinced he must have imagined it.

'I mean, is it even *legal*? To keep a lion as a pet. It can't be.'

'It is, sir,' Wogan said. 'I have a special licence.'

'A LICENCE? A LION LICENCE? I mean . . . of all the . . . Well . . . GET THAT LION OUT OF HERE! THIS INSTANT! If the school inspectors find out about this, we're in big trouble!'

'OK, sir. If you say so.'

Mr Wind turned and walked away, shaking his head and muttering to himself about lion licences. The moment he'd turned the corner, Charlie the lion turned back to normal-Charlie.

'I can't believe,' Flora said to Wogan after a long pause, 'you actually got away with that.'

'I was completely confident,' Wogan replied, nonchalantly. 'I knew it would work.'[32]

'Anyway!' said Flora, after giving Wogan a final disbelieving stare. 'We need to find Dylan again! And somehow get into that basement!'

They hurried back to the disco, but just outside the hall they bumped into Daisy and Lola.

---

[32] This was a lie. And a big fat one, as well.

'Ah!' said Lola. 'There you all are. We were just looking for you.'

'We thought you'd want this,' said Daisy, holding up a key. 'It fell out of Dylan's pocket when he was doing the headspin. You know, during the dance-off. I picked it up – thought it might be useful for you.'

She handed the key to Flora and walked off, arm in arm with Lola, leaving the four friends slack-jawed and gobsmacked.

After a moment of stunned silence, Flora snapped.

'Quick – split up, guys!' she shouted. 'Wogan! Take the key and go with Mohsen to check the animals are safe! Charlie, you come with me and let's stop Dylan showing the video!'

Wogan and Mohsen raced off, and Charlie and Flora plunged into the hall.

But despite frantic searching, they couldn't find Dylan anywhere. The flashing lights and dancing crowds didn't make their job any easier. Five fruitless minutes later, they stood in the middle of the dance floor in despair.

'I'm done for,' Charlie shouted over the music. 'He's won.'

Flora looked at Charlie, lost for words.

Wogan and Mohsen suddenly ran up so fast, they nearly bowled them over like skittles.

'We were right!' panted Mohsen. 'He DOES have the animals down there! It's absolutely full of them! It's like Noah's Ark!'

'Oh my gosh, I knew it!' gasped Flora.

'Did you see the Great Catsby?' asked Charlie, urgently.

'No,' replied Mohsen. 'I'm afraid not. But it was dark, I might have missed —'

Suddenly the music cut out and a voice came booming through the speakers.

'Ladies and gentlemen, can I have your attention, please?'

The voice echoed round the hall. Everyone was craning their heads trying to see who it belonged to. Charlie, Flora, Mohsen and Wogan didn't have to crane their heads though – they knew.

And sure enough, stepping on to the stage, carrying a microphone, was Dylan.

'Ladies and gentlemen,' he continued. 'A monster has been walking among us.'

The audience murmured in surprise.

'Have any of you noticed how animals have been going missing around town? From the zoo? From your own homes?'

Everybody muttered and nodded – they *had* noticed. 'Well, I am here to reveal what has happened to those poor creatures.'

Behind Dylan, the projector screen flickered into life.

'We have to stop him!' cried Flora.

'How?' asked Charlie.

But Flora didn't reply. She was out of ideas.

'I'm afraid,' Dylan continued, 'I have to tell you that your cute kitties and pretty pooches won't be coming back. They've been *eaten*!'

The audience gasped.

'Yes, every last one of them has been eaten. By a monstrous freak!'

The audience gasped again.

Dylan clicked a remote control in his hand and on the big screen that hung over the stage

appeared a shaky image of Charlie's front door.
Dylan's finger hovered over the 'play' button.

'And,' Dylan announced, 'that monster is –'

'Mehehehehehehehehehehehehehh!'

The strange sound came from behind the
black-out curtain at the back of the stage.

It sounded very much like an animal.

Some titters rippled through the crowd of
children on the dance floor.

Dylan ignored them.

'That monster is –'

'Mehehehehehehehehehehehehehe!'

And then, from behind Dylan, blinking in the light, a goat slowly trotted out on to the stage.

Dylan turned round and scowled.

'Charlie . . . ?' Dylan said to the goat. 'Is that you?'

The crowd burst into wild laughter.

'Wogan,' said Charlie. 'Can I just check . . . Did you close the basement door behind you?'

'Did I . . . close the . . . errmmmm,' Wogan scratched his head and eyed Mohsen nervously. 'I thiiiiiiiiiiink so. Moh?'

'I . . . errr,' said Mohsen. 'I can't say I'm *one hundred* per cent certain we did.'

And at that moment, chaos broke out.

Puffin Books

80 Strand

London

Dear Mr Copeland,

There is only one chapter to go! WHERE ARE
THE MAMMOTHS?! CHARLIE BETTER
TURN INTO A MAMMOTH IN THE NEXT
FEW PAGES OR ... OR ... WOE BETIDE YOU!

Yours sincerely,

The Publisher

Dear Puffin Books,

Relax! Charlie is totally going to change into
a mammoth any minute now. It's going to be an
awesome climax.

Yours truthfully,

Sam Copeland

P.S. I bet you don't even know what 'woe betide
you' means.

CHAPTER 14

It was the eagles that started it.

Two great birds they were, with huge talons and vicious beaks that looked like they could devour a small child in minutes flat. And there was something in their cold, hard eyes which suggested that was exactly what was on their minds.

They swooped out from behind the stage and circled the gawping crowd of children, who seemed to think that this might be part of the entertainment.

A second later they realized it most certainly wasn't.

The eagles swooped down to attack.

Fortunately, the teachers' heads were closest to the eagles' clutching talons. Miss Fyre let out a great scream as one of them became tangled in her hair. Mr Wind came running towards her, flapping his arms.

'Get back, you feathery fiends!' he screeched. 'Leave her alone, you demonic dive-bombers!'

The children began to panic, screaming and running blindly in every direction.

Next came two dozen cats and dogs of all shapes and sizes. The dogs barked and yapped, racing round the hall like mad things, while the cats scrambled up the curtains, yowling and looking every bit as panicked as the children. The goat kept bleating furiously from the stage, seemingly enjoying the chaos below. Next to the goat stood Dylan, staring in horror at what was unfolding.

As Charlie watched, Dylan jumped down from the stage and began sneaking his way towards the exit. The missing chinchillas had now joined the party and were running between the screaming children's feet. Meanwhile, the goat had followed Dylan off the stage and was now merrily butting the bums of anyone who came near it, knocking some of the Year 2s clear into the air.

Between the yapping dogs and the dive-bombing eagles, the butting goat, the screeching cats and the squeaking chinchillas, there seemed to be no escape.

The dogs were chasing the cats and now the cats began chasing the chinchillas, which caused even more chaos. The hall was a whirling, barking, screaming tornado of terrified children, panicking teachers and animals going bananas.

'See if you can calm things down,' Charlie yelled to his friends. 'I've got a job to do.'

Charlie forced his way through the crowd after Dylan. It was hard to make any progress, though. Everyone in the hall was just running round in circles.

Why isn't anybody leaving? thought Charlie.

A moment later, he found out.

He and Dylan were approaching the main doors, which should have been the obvious way out for the panicking children.

There, blocking the doorway, wonky yellow teeth bared, was the missing llama. It looked *distinctly* unhappy at having been locked in a basement, and seemed to be scanning the crowd for the boy who had done it.

As soon as its gaze fell on Dylan, the llama's dark eyes narrowed. Dylan screeched to a halt. The llama pawed the ground for a moment, like an angry bull – then charged.

With a high-pitched scream of terror, Dylan fled. The llama gave chase, scattering children hither and thither.

Miss Fyre – hair a tangled mess – and Mr Wind – eyes on stalks – were running round like their bums were on fire, trying to shepherd the children to safety, but the animals were everywhere and still more kept appearing – ones which Charlie had no idea had been missing.

Parrots and cockatoos flew overhead, flashes of colour flitting between the lasers, pooping on people below. A huge monitor lizard was skittering and sliding along the floor. Two capybaras were chewing on the black-out curtains. A herd of majestic stick insects was sweeping across the dance floor but nobody noticed them because they looked like sticks.

How did Dylan manage to steal all these animals? thought Charlie as he stalked him through the crowd. Well, there was only one way of finding out.

Now the llama had left its post at the exit,

Dylan had managed to sneak back round, out through the doors and down the corridor. He legged it past the staff room with Charlie in hot pursuit.

'Dylan!' called Charlie. 'Stop!'

Dylan swung around wildly. When he saw Charlie, he grimaced. But then a wide smile broke across his face.

'Aww,' said Dylan. 'So cute!'

Charlie was somewhat surprised by Dylan's unexpected compliment.

'Well, uh, thanks, Dylan, that's really nice of you but –'

'Not you, imbecile! Behind you!' Dylan sneered, pointing.

Charlie turned to find a pair of penguins a few metres away. His first thought was they were indeed very cute. But then he remembered what the penguins at the zoo had been like. There was something *odd* about the way these birds were waddling towards them. There was a determination in that waddle, a cold, blood-thirsty look in their eyes.

These penguins were looking for revenge.

And hell hath no fury like a penguin scorned.

'Dylan!' Charlie shouted. 'Run!'

'Run?' replied Dylan incredulously. 'From these adorable penguins?'

'They are not adorable! They're vicious! Just trust me and *run*!'

The boys both began running and, with a blood-chilling squawk, the penguins gave chase, waddling after them with unnatural speed.

Charlie and Dylan raced into the school kitchen and slammed the door behind them. They bolted to the end of the long stainless-steel counter and hid under it, panting heavily.

After a moment, they lifted their heads and looked back at the door. A beak suddenly appeared at a window, followed by an emotionless, malevolent eye, scanning the kitchen for the boys.

The boys ducked back into their hiding-place.

'We're safe in here, aren't we?' Dylan asked, terrified.

'Yes,' replied Charlie. 'Unless they've figured out how to open doors.'

Suddenly the door handle rattled.

And slowly the door creaked open.

'Clever girl . . .' Charlie whispered to himself, with a grimace of admiration.

And then came the sound of scaly feet slowly slapping against the floor.

The penguins were in the kitchen.

The slapping came closer.

Slap.

And closer.

Slap.

Charlie pointed, indicating to Dylan that

they should split up. Dylan nodded and they both skittered across the floor, trying to keep their heads down.

Charlie clambered into a small cupboard full of pots and pans, and slid the door closed, leaving it open a crack so he could just see out.

He couldn't tell where Dylan had hidden.

The sound of his own breathing was deafening inside the cupboard.

Slap.

They were coming towards him.

Slap.

Suddenly, the open beak of one of the penguins appeared in the crack of the open door, snapping viciously. Charlie flinched, terrified, pressing himself further back into the cupboard.

They had him trapped.

He was done for –

'Ooh look! Penguins!' Charlie heard a girl's voice cry from the far end of the kitchen.

'I love penguins!' replied another.

Charlie heard the girls approaching. And then he saw them – it was Daisy and Lola. They were trying to pet the penguins!

'Noooo!' Charlie cried, jumping out of the cupboard. 'Run!'

Daisy and Lola nearly collapsed in fright.

'Charlie? What on *earth* are you doing hiding in the cupboard?' Daisy asked.

'The . . . p-p-penguins,' he replied.

'What do you mean?' said Lola, in disbelief. 'You were hiding from the penguins?'

Charlie was starting to feel more than a little embarrassed.

'They're . . . dangerous,' he replied uncertainly.

'What are you talking about?' said Daisy, patting the head of one of the birds. 'Penguins aren't dangerous, they're adorable.'

And then Daisy and Lola grabbed a penguin each by the flipper, and walked them out of the kitchen.

'Such a strange boy,' said Lola as they went.

Daisy nodded. 'I really don't think Wogan should hang around with him any more.'

For a moment, Charlie couldn't quite remember why he'd been so terrified of the small black-and-white birds. Then, just as it was going out through the door, one of the

penguins glanced back over its shoulder with a look of such deep hatred and fury it gave Charlie the chills.

And then Lola, Daisy and the two penguins were gone, and Charlie was alone with Dylan.

'You can come out now, it's safe,' Charlie said.

Dylan climbed out of the huge bin he had been hiding in. He was covered in potato peelings and half-eaten broccoli.

'If you tell anybody I was hiding in there because of *penguins* –' Dylan began.

'I won't,' Charlie said.

'I mean, why were we even running away from them in the first place?' asked Dylan. 'Couldn't you have just changed into an animal and scared them away? It would have made for a more exciting ending to this whole . . .' Dylan waved his hand in the air. '*Thing.*'

Charlie didn't have an answer for that. He had just thought of a different ending.

'Dylan?' he asked.

'What,' asked Dylan grumpily, wiping bits of food off himself.

'Will you join our gang?'

'What?' Dylan replied, a look of utter disbelief on his mucky face.

'I've been thinking. Will you join our gang?' he repeated.

Charlie had *indeed* been thinking.

He'd been thinking about how Dylan had come to the school dance and stood in the corner alone, without a friend in the world. Charlie couldn't remember the last time he'd seen Dylan play with *anybody*. Dylan was always on his own. And thinking about that made Charlie's heart ache.

Charlie remembered, now, that he had been great friends with Dylan before the Great Snail Race. And how he had felt bad for a long time after their friendship ended but had forced himself to ignore those feelings, and then eventually ignore Dylan.

And he remembered that, no matter how bad things were for him at home, at least he had his friends to talk to. Dylan had nobody.

'Why would I join your stupid gang? You just want to keep me quiet and make sure I don't tell anyone your secret, don't you?' snapped Dylan.

'I don't care about that any more,' said Charlie, and he finally meant it. 'Tell people if you want. My brother nearly died. My family nearly lost all our money. And now my parents are separating. Bad things happen – and I can deal with it. We used to be friends, Dylan. I want to be friends again.'

Dylan stayed silent, picking at a bit of skin on his thumb.

'I treated you badly in the past and I want to make it up to you. I know things are tough for you, Dylan,' continued Charlie. 'And you know they are for me. We should stick together. Come on. Join our gang. Please.'

Dylan looked up at Charlie and his eyes were glistening with tears.

'Do you really want me to?' Dylan asked.

Charlie nodded, not trusting that his voice wouldn't crack.

'This isn't a joke?' Dylan asked.

Charlie shook his head, his heart a confused mess of joy and sadness.

'What will Flora and Mohsen and Wogan say? They won't like it,' said Dylan.

Charlie smiled. 'They probably won't. To begin with. But they will eventually.'

'In that case,' Dylan said, 'I'd love to join your gang!'

Dylan stuck out a hand for Charlie to shake and Charlie surprised himself by instead pulling Dylan into a hug and slapping him on the back.

'Here you are!' came a sudden voice. 'We've been looking every– Hang about, what are you doing?'

It was Wogan, and closely following behind were Flora and Mohsen.

'Were you hugging *him*?' asked Wogan, a look of horror on his face as he pointed at Dylan.

'Well, this is quite the turn-up for the books,' said Mohsen.

'Yup. Dylan is joining our gang,' said Charlie, bracing himself for a barrage of protests.

There was a moment's silence. Then . . .

'I think that is an *excellent* idea,' said Flora simply.

Charlie's jaw dropped.

'Welcome to our gang, Dylan.' Flora shook Dylan's hand.

Dylan looked like he had just seen a ghost riding the Loch Ness monster waving a cowboy hat over his head.

'What about you guys?' Charlie asked Wogan and Mohsen. 'You OK with it too?'

'If you're happy, Charlie, then I'm happy,' said Mohsen. 'Welcome to the gang, Dylan.'

'And you?' Charlie looked at Wogan. 'What do you think?'

Wogan's answer seemed to take an age to come.

'I think Dylan is a big clodhopping ninny-head who looks like a wet stick of seven-day-old celery,' Wogan said. 'And I think you,' he continued, pointing at Charlie, 'have completely lost your marbles.'

Dylan looked crestfallen.

'Having said that . . .' Wogan said slowly. 'Maybe a fifth member of our team wouldn't be SO bad. Suppose we *could* start a five-a-side squad.'

'So, all agreed then?' asked Flora, grinning. 'Dylan to join our gang?'

'Agreed!' they chorused.

And Charlie saw something he hadn't seen for a long time – Dylan was wearing a broad smile. Dylan was *happy*.

'Well then,' said Flora. 'The first job for this newly-expanded gang is Operation Clean-Up – we've got a lot of animals to capture! It's WILD out there!'

'That's a point actually,' said Charlie. 'Dylan, how *did* you get them all into school in the first place?'

'Ah!' said Dylan, waggling his eyebrows. 'Now that's a secret!'

'Fine!' Charlie laughed. 'But what on earth were you going to do with them all afterwards?'

Dylan grinned sheepishly and shrugged. 'To be honest, I hadn't really thought that far ahead . . .'

Charlie grinned back, but then it dropped from his face. He had one more urgent question.

'Dylan, do you really not know where the Great Catsby is?'

Dylan shook his head. 'I'm sorry, Charlie. I didn't take him. I promise. I don't know where he is.'

Charlie fell silent. That meant the Great Catsby really *was* missing.

Where *was* he?

***

By the time the parents came to pick up their children from the dance, most of the animals had been captured and temporarily put back into the basement until they could be returned to their rightful owners. The friends were all covered in cuts and scratches, feathers and bits of fluff. Miss Fyre and Mr Wind were huddled in a corner, looking shell-shocked.

Charlie's mum was the first of the gang's

parents to turn up to collect.

'Can I just say goodbye to my friends?' Charlie said to her.

'Of course,' she replied with a soft smile.

Charlie went over to the others. 'OK, guys, I've got to go.'

'Wait, Charlie. Let me show you something,' Dylan said, pulling his phone out of his pocket.

He opened his videos and started pressing keys. 'That's it,' he said. 'I've deleted the video of you changing. Your secret is safe with me.'

'Thanks,' said Charlie. 'And we all agree we're never going to tell anyone it was Dylan who stole all the animals, right, guys?'

The gang all nodded vigorously.

'So, all's well that ends well!' said Mohsen cheerily.

A brief smile flickered on Charlie's face but then he saw his mother. She was standing alone on the empty dance floor, spotlights sweeping around her.

'Not exactly,' Charlie muttered.

The last night had ended.

Tomorrow his life would change forever when his dad left.

Flora stepped up to Charlie and took his hand.

'We'll be here for you.'

And one by one his friends came up to Charlie and hugged him.

Dylan was the last to give him a hug. As he did, he whispered in Charlie's ear.

'We'll be strong, Charlie. Together.'

And as Charlie walked over to his mum, he was glad the hall was still dark enough to hide his tears.

EPILOGUE[33]

Sometimes, Charlie thought, *life picks you up, shakes you like a baby with a rattle, then drops you on your bum, and there's not a single thing you can do about it.* That's what he had learned: you can change some things, but with others all you can do is try to accept them.

And his dad packing the last of his things in the small removal van parked outside their house was the latest part of life he just had to accept. It was sad – *he* was sad – and that was all right. It was OK to be sad, sometimes.

---

[33] An epilogue sounds like something you would produce on the toilet after you hadn't done a poo in ages and then had a big curry. But it isn't. An epilogue is a final conclusion to a story. It's basically just a fancy word for the last chapter.

His dad slammed the van door shut, came up to Charlie and squatted down on his haunches.

'That's the lot, son. You doing OK?'

Charlie nodded.

'Yes, Dad.'

And Charlie nearly was.

SmoothMove came up behind him.

'OK, Dad. We'll see you next weekend, yeah?'

'That's right. I'll have your new bedroom sorted for you. OK, boys. Look after your mum for me.'

And with a last hug, Charlie's dad got into the van and drove off, leaving the two boys standing next to each other in the early-morning drizzle.

'Come on then,' said SmoothMove, putting his arm round Charlie. 'Let's get in out of the rain.'

Charlie nodded, the rain washing away his tears. When he turned around, there was his mum waiting for him, arms open. Charlie ran and buried himself into the hug.

★★★

Later that day, though, something extraordinary happened, which finally gave Charlie his smile back.

Charlie had been playing FIFA with SmoothMove (and *almost* beating him), and afterwards he went up to his bedroom. As usual,

Chairman Meow was sitting on top of the laundry basket and something niggled at Charlie's memory.

Charlie shut the door and quickly changed into a cat.

'Oh, how marvellous,' Chairman Meow said, in a voice dripping with sarcasm. 'You're back.'

'Chairman Meow,' Charlie said, ignoring his mocking. 'You said before that you knew where the Great Catsby – the cat who sits in boxes – went. Would you *please* tell me?'

Chairman Meow thought for a while, licked himself, and then said:

'If I do, you must do something for me in return.'

'What?' Charlie asked.

'First, you must agree to bathe more than once a week. The smell of you is indescribably awful. It causes my nose actual physical pain and –'

'Fine!' Charlie snapped.

'Second, I want you to promise never to change into a cat ever again.'

'OK, agreed —'

'You see, if you're human, it's easier for me to pretend you don't exist. You're the most tedious creature I have ever had the misfortune —'

'OK, OK!' Charlie flashed. 'I've already agreed! Believe me, I'm in absolutely no rush to talk to you again. You're the rudest, most — *Anyway*,' Charlie said, trying to control his temper. 'Tell me what you know. Where is the Great Catsby?'

'He's beneath me,' Chairman Meow said, licking a paw.

Charlie rolled his eyes.

'There's no need to be mean,' he said.

'No, he's right beneath me,' replied Chairman Meow.

'What do you mean? Like downstairs?!'

'No. He's *literally* beneath me. In this basket. I've had him trapped here for days.'

'WHAT?!' exclaimed Charlie. 'WHY WOULD YOU DO THAT?'

'You will never understand the workings of the feline brain,' Chairman Meow replied haughtily. 'My reasons will be forever beyond your tiny monkey-mind. But basically, I did it because it was funny.'

'WHAT IS WRONG WITH YOU? YOU ARE ACTUALLY THE WORST ANIMAL IN THE WHOLE WORLD.'[34]

Charlie immediately changed back into Charlie. Chairman Meow jumped off the laundry basket and stalked out of the room.

Charlie lifted the lid and, sure enough, curled up in a ball inside, was the Great Catsby. He blinked in the light, then jumped out and

---

[34] Apart from penguins. And puffins.

ran downstairs, presumably very hungry.

The next day at lunch, Charlie told the gang – Flora, Mohsen, Wogan and Dylan – how Chairman Meow had been keeping the Great Catsby prisoner the whole time.

'I knew it!' said Wogan, thumping his palm.[35]

'OK, guys, actually I lied, I didn't know.'[36]

---

[35] I think by now you probably realize there is a very slim chance that Wogan did actually know. But that's the thing with Wogan – sometimes he can surprise you. Let's trust him this time, shall we?

[36] Gah, Wogan! That's the LAST time we're going to believe you.

Charlie was happy to be with his friends but inside he was feeling very conflicted.

'I feel very conflicted,' he said, as if he was reading the mind of the narrator.

Charlie would be staying over at his dad's new flat for the first time that weekend, which he was very excited about. But he was also sad because his friends had organized a play date on the Sunday morning and Charlie couldn't come because his dad couldn't afford a car yet and the new flat was miles away.

Charlie was about to explain to his friends why he was feeling conflicted, but the narrator had just done it for him, so there was no need.

Flora waggled her eyebrows. She had a plan.

And her plan was this: if Charlie –

'I have a plan,' Flora said, rudely interrupting the narrator. 'And the plan is this . . .'

★★★

Charlie's weekend with his dad and SmoothMove was great fun. On Saturday, they all went to the cinema to see the latest Star Wars movie, and then had curry for dinner.

Their dad's new flat was small but, much to Charlie and SmoothMove's surprise, it was fun sharing a room. Charlie kept changing into different animals to surprise SmoothMove and they giggled until late into the night.

The next morning, Charlie was woken by rain hammering on the skylight above his head. He got up, wolfed his breakfast and sidled up to his dad.

'Daaaad . . . ?'

'Yes, son?' his dad smiled.

'Can I go and explore the area? There's a park with a playground down the road.'

'Okey-dokey. Make sure you're back for lunch, yes?'

Charlie nodded vigorously, put his trainers

on, rushed out the door, ran down a side street, and hid behind a large bin. Making sure nobody was watching, Charlie closed his eyes and changed.

For a moment, Charlie stood, feeling the rain on his back. Then he stretched his great wings, and arced his head up to the sky.

A few flaps and Charlie was in the air. He circled, getting his bearings. Flora's house was on the other side of town, so he had to cross the busy centre.

Charlie beat his wings – once, twice – and he soared higher into the sky, the wind whistling through his silver-white feathers, now glistening wet.

He arrowed gracefully onwards, towards a thick cloud which hung over the town.

Over the sound of wind and rain came a sudden, startling voice from just below him – a voice Charlie immediately recognized.

'Charlie
BranMuffin! It
is I, Jean-Claude
the pigeon!'

Charlie looked down, and there, flying underneath him, were three birds he knew very well.

'And it is I, Antoine the pigeon! You may 'ave changed your appearance, Snarly CrackBuffin, but we know it is you!'

'And you are more beautiful than ever!' said the third pigeon. 'What a glorious white pigeon with a strange long neck you 'ave become!'

'We shall join you on your journey!'

'We shall protect
you from dangers untold!'

'We shall seek crumbs!'

'Onwards! Forever onwards!'

They flanked Charlie on either side, wing-tip to wing-tip. More and more pigeons joined them on their way, until Charlie was at the tip of a huge V-formation, stretching across the heavy grey sky.

On Charlie flew, through the lashing rain, towards his friends, and towards a life he did not yet know.

Puffin Books

80 Strand

London

Dear Mr Copeland,

We despise you.

    Yours NOT faithfully,

    The Publisher

Dear Puffin Books,

Not as much as I despise you.

    Yours dishonestly,

    Sam Copeland

Dear Sam Copeland,

I don't like you either.

    The absolute worstest wishes,

    Josh, nine, Whitstable

Dear Josh from Whitstable,

No one asked you. You're the worst, Josh from Whitstable.

Even worsest wishes, times infinity,
Sam Copeland

Dear Sam Copeland,

Loved this book. I've read ALL the books. No one knows books more than me. And this is the best story ever! Awesome!

D. Trump, 73 and ¾, USA

Dear D. Trump,

Thanks! Did you know that in Britain, 'trump' is another word for 'fart'?

Best wishes,
Sam Copeland

Dear Sam Copeland,

I hate you.

D. Trump, 73 and ¾, USA

Read how Charlie's adventures began

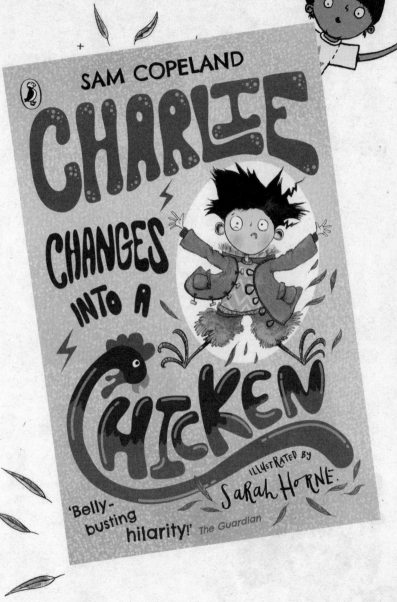

SAM COPELAND

CHARLIE

CHANGES
INTO A

CHICKEN

ILLUSTRATED BY
SARAH HORNE

'Belly-
busting
hilarity!' The Guardian

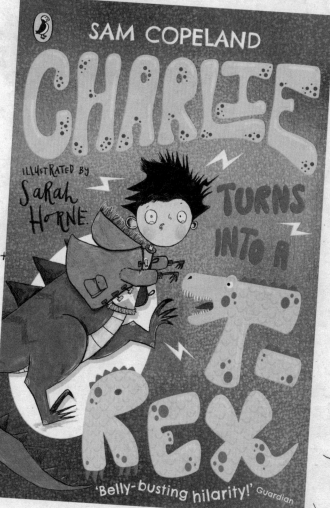

SAM COPELAND

CHARLIE

ILLUSTRATED BY
SARAH HORNE

TURNS
INTO A
T-REX

'Belly-busting hilarity!' Guardian

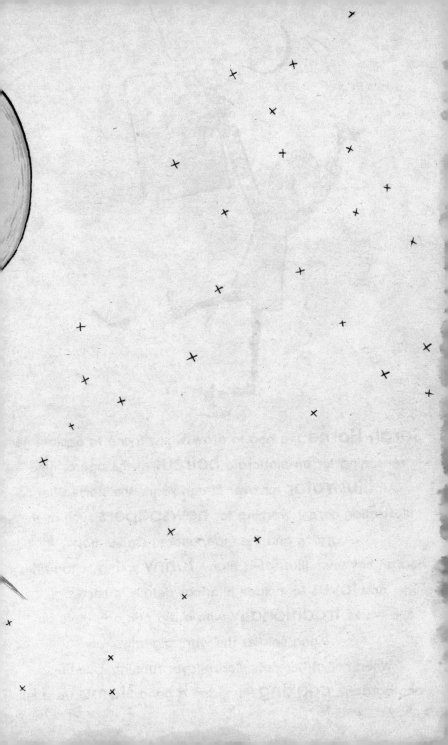

Sarah Horne learned to draw whilst trying to explain her reasoning for an elaborate **haircut** at the age of nine. An **illustrator** for over fifteen years, she started her Illustration career working for **newspapers** such as the *Guardian* and the *Independent On Sunday*. Sarah has since illustrated many **funny** young fiction titles and **loves** to include hilarious details in her work. She works **traditionally** with a dip pen and Indian ink, and finishes the work digitally. When not at her desk, Sarah loves running, painting, photography, **cooking**, film, and a good **stomp** up a hill.